"Let us in, please!"

Before Adam could respond, the sound of gunshots exploded through his speakers.

More gunshots sounded and the woman's screams were more desperate now.

Although every instinct screamed hide, he couldn't ignore her. He took a deep breath and pressed a button. The gate swung inward, and he called through the intercom. "Come in."

Caught off balance, the woman fell forward, twisting her body as she hit the ground. She rolled sideways and he caught a glimpse of a bundle wrapped in a blanket. Was she holding a baby?

By the time Adam managed to get to the front door and fling it open, the woman, child and baby were making their way up the path. He stepped out on the porch.

"Come inside. You'll be safe here."

He ushered them inside and shut the door firmly behind him.

The woman's whole body sagged in relief. "Thank you for letting us in. I don't know what we would have done—"

Another shot sounded from outside, followed by the sound of shattering glass.

Cate Nolan lives in New York City, but she escapes to the ocean any chance she gets. Once school is done for the day, Cate loves to leave her real life behind and play with the characters in her imagination. She's got that suspense-writer gene that sees danger and a story in everyday occurrences. Cate particularly loves to write stories of faith enabling ordinary people to overcome extraordinary danger. You can find her at www.catenolanauthor.com.

Books by Cate Nolan

Love Inspired Suspense

Christmas in Hiding
Texas Witness Threat
Colorado Mountain Kidnapping

Visit the Author Profile page at LoveInspired.com.

Colorado Mountain Kidnapping

CATE NOLAN

LOVE INSPIRED SUSPENSE

INSPIRATIONAL ROMANCE

LOVE INSPIRED® SUSPENSE
INSPIRATIONAL ROMANCE

ISBN-13: 978-1-335-59820-2

Colorado Mountain Kidnapping

Recycling programs for this product may not exist in your area.

Love Inspired
22 Adelaide St. West, 41st Floor
Toronto, Ontario M5H 4E3, Canada
www.LoveInspired.com

Printed in Lithuania

MIX
Paper | Supporting responsible forestry
FSC® C021394

But they that wait upon the Lord shall renew their
strength; they shall mount up with wings as eagles;
they shall run, and not be weary;
and they shall walk, and not faint.

—*Isaiah* 40:31

For my daughters, Nora and Aislinn. You are my world. Thank you for all your love and support as I worked on this book.

And for Fenway, my faithful muse who crossed the rainbow bridge while I was writing it. I love to imagine you running along the beach with Daddy.

And finally, to those who gave all in service of their country, and for those who bear the scars.

ONE

Isabelle Weaver was fighting fatigue as she snuggled on the sofa with her five-year-old daughter Mia. Snow drifted softly past the window of her friend Jess's cozy cabin shrouding her view of the mountains. Isabelle yawned. After an exhausting day of entertaining two children while her friend had some appointments, Isabelle deeply appreciated the early evening calm. Jess's baby was finally sleeping peacefully in her crib in the bedroom, and Mia was drawing pictures of snowmen. Isabelle sipped her tea and sighed contentedly. Colorado in January was an entirely new experience for her. She pulled her heavy sweater closer around her shoulders and was just contemplating lighting a fire to ward off the chill when her ringtone abruptly shattered the silence.

Isabelle grabbed for her phone, trying to answer before the baby woke. Seeing her friend's name on the display, she spoke quietly. "Jess, where are you? I was getting worried—"

Jess cut her off almost at once. "Take the girls. Get out of the house—immediately."

"What? Is this a joke? What's going on?" But Isabelle sensed the answer even before Jess replied. Her friend sounded out of breath, terror threaded through her voice.

"No joke. Go."

"Where are you? Let me call for help."

For a moment, Isabelle heard nothing but Jess's raspy breath. "Isa, go. It's life or death. If—"

A gunshot exploded in the distance. Isabelle froze. Had she heard that through the phone or from outside?

"Jess?"

"If I don't make it back, protect Laura. The lawyer in Breckenridge has guardianship papers." Jess's voice lowered to a choked whisper. "Make sure she knows I love her."

"Jess—"

"Isa, go now!"

A squeal of tires and another gunshot sounded in Isabelle's ear before the phone went dead.

"Mama, is Aunt Jess coming home now?"

Before she could even think how to answer her daughter's question, Isabelle heard car wheels crunching on the gravel driveway. Though a part of her brain wanted to hope it was Jess, her gut said otherwise.

Mia jumped up. "Aunt Jess." She ran for the door.

"Mia, no!"

Isabelle launched herself off the sofa, managing to grasp her daughter's arm just before she reached the door. She put a finger to her lips and slid along the wall to the window so she could peer out from behind the heavy winter drapes.

Just as she'd feared, it was not Jess's car.

Doors opened on both sides and two men emerged.

With guns.

"Mia, come with me right now." Her harsh whisper must have conveyed the seriousness because her daughter didn't protest. Isabelle's heart broke as she took in Mia's frightened expression. She crouched down beside her. "Aunt Jess asked us to take Laura and go out the back. We have to be very quiet, so we don't wake Laura."

Mia's face brightened and Isabelle knew she'd concluded that this was a game. Maybe it would be best to let her think that.

"But, Mama—"

Fists pounded the door.

Isabelle didn't hesitate. As she grabbed their jackets off the hook, Mia reached for hers. "I can do it, Mama."

Isabelle put her finger to her lips as a reminder. Mia nodded and grinned. Isabelle guided her into the bedroom. She took a moment to stuff her phone into her jeans' pocket before crossing to the window. "I'll help you climb out and then hand Laura to you. Wait for me. I'll be right behind you."

Isabelle's heart was thumping as she struggled with a sash that felt like it had been painted shut. Rising panic fueled her efforts as she took a deep breath and put everything she had into a mighty shove. The sash went sailing up. *Please, Lord, don't let the men have heard that.*

Heart in her throat, Isabelle stuck her head out to make sure she wasn't delivering her daughter into danger. There was no sign of the men, so he turned and gave Mia a kiss before whispering, "Remember, we have to be very quiet. We don't want to wake Laura."

Mia smiled impishly and held her finger over her lips before she scrambled over the ledge and dropped to the snowy ground.

Isabelle pulled her own coat on, then turned to scoop the sleeping baby from the crib. She swaddled the blankets around her, creating a sling she then used to lower her into Mia's arms.

Please, Lord, let Laura stay asleep. A crying baby would give them away in a heartbeat.

Once Mia had the baby securely in her arms, Isabelle glanced back. She scanned the room as she tried to focus her scrambled thoughts.

The banging on the door sounded like they'd break through any minute. It underscored the panic ringing through her body. She needed her purse and her car keys, but they were on the kitchen counter. There was no time to go back for them. _Life or death_, she reminded herself as she climbed over the ledge. Her fingers were still gripping the sill when she heard something crash against the front door.

Isabelle dropped to the ground and took Laura from Mia. "We have to run as fast as we can to the tree house, okay?"

Mia nodded and took off across the snow-covered yard. Isabelle ran closely behind her, making a beeline for the trees. Terror dogged her steps. Her breaths came in heavy gasps as the baby weighed down her arms and she struggled to keep herself between Mia and the line of sight of anyone in the house.

She needed to call for help, but she didn't dare stop. If she could reach the tree line, she'd have time to call the sheriff. Another loud crash sounded from the house, followed by angry voices. Isabelle's heart sank.

"Mama, who is that?"

The tremor in Mia's voice escalated the fear coursing through Isabelle's body. "Ignore them, baby. We have to keep running."

They reached the tree line and Isabelle bent over, gasping for breath. The baby whimpered, and Isabelle wanted to moan in unison. Instead, she wrapped the blanket more securely and tucked Laura into a football hold.

Only then did she dare a look back, at which point she nearly collapsed in despair. Their footsteps shone like an arrow across the snow, pointing in the direction they'd traveled.

Isabelle's limbs felt paralyzed, and she had to fight through the terror that was numbing her brain. What should she do? How could she protect these children?

She was mere feet from the tree house, but that wouldn't

be a refuge now that the men could see where she'd gone. She needed to keep running. But first she had to call for help—now, before the men followed her trail.

Isabelle reached into her pocket for her phone, hoping to at least have time to get through to a 9-1-1 operator, but her hand came up empty.

Her phone must have fallen from her pocket as she'd climbed out the window.

Despair snowballed, colder than this Colorado winter. Shouts from the house made it clear she couldn't go back. One man stood at the window gesturing and shouting to another who had just rounded the corner.

A shot rang out behind her. Bark splintered off a tree and sliced across her shoulder. Isabelle's terror ratcheted up. How could she possibly protect Mia and Laura with men shooting at them?

Isabelle squeezed her eyes shut. *Dear Lord, help us.* Another shot cracked the air and Isabelle felt the impact as it shattered a branch above her head, dumping snow down on them.

Mia whimpered. "Mommy, I'm scared. I don't like this game."

Isabelle's heart cracked. In a perfect world, she could take the time to comfort her daughter, but then, in a perfect world, no one would be shooting at them. Keeping the girls alive took priority for now. She hardened her resolve as she wrapped her free arm around Mia's shoulders and guided her behind a tree. "We have to pray to Jesus to help us, sweetie," she whispered. "Remember the prayer I taught you? 'Jesus, I trust in you.' Just keep saying it over and over."

As Mia repeated the prayer, Isabelle quickly studied their surroundings. There was less snow cover in the woods. Maybe she could find a path that wouldn't show their footsteps so clearly.

She grasped Mia's hand and started off at an angle opposite to where she'd been headed. She tried to step on the leaves and pine needles as much as possible. Praying that the motion would keep Laura calm, she and Mia quickly made their way from one cluster of trees to another.

When she felt like she couldn't take another step because of the stitch in her side, she stopped to listen. She could hear the voices still, but they sounded far off. Had the gunmen lost their track?

The thought no sooner crossed her mind than she heard another shot fired in the air, but it didn't hit anything near her and the children. Hoping they were just trying to flush her out, Isabelle trudged on. There was a break in the woods up ahead, and she could just make out a fence, one of those stockade types that looked like it was meant to keep the world out. If only she could find a way behind it. She leaned down and whispered to Mia, "See that fence? We're going to go there and try to get inside."

Mia's eyes widened with fear. Isabelle's heart ached. She'd do anything to replace that fear with the laughter and joy she usually saw. And she would. As soon as they were safe.

Mia tugged on her arm, keeping her from moving forward.

"Come, sweetie. We have to go behind the fence."

"No." Mia dug her heels in. "The scary man lives there."

Isabelle cast a glance over her shoulder. "What scary man?"

Mia wrapped her arms around Isabelle's leg as she replied. "I heard Aunt Jess tell you he's like the billy goats. They're scary."

Another time, she would have laughed, but now Mia's words gave her pause. When Jess had said her neighbor was reclusive and gruff, Isabelle had assumed he was just someone who cherished his privacy. Could Jess have meant something worse?

Close by—too close—a branch cracked and footsteps crunched through the frozen undergrowth. Isabelle's heart sank as she heard the man call to his partner. Their path had been discovered.

If her choice was an unfriendly neighbor or men with guns, the answer was obvious. She didn't care how gruff he was if he would only let them shelter behind his fence until she could call for help.

"Mia, we don't have a choice right now. Run!"

Isabelle shifted Laura in her arms, urged Mia forward, and made a dash for the fence. *Please God, let someone be home*—even if he wasn't nice.

They ran through the snow, looking for a gate, but there was no break in the long fence. Isabelle was ready to collapse in exhaustion by the time they rounded the corner. A groan escaped her lips as she saw nothing but another lengthy wood wall ahead. She paused for a breath, taking solace in the knowledge that the men in pursuit hadn't broken through into the clearing yet.

"I can't run any more, Mama."

"Just a little bit more, baby. We're almost there." They had to be. Somewhere along this fence there had to be a gate, didn't there?

"Come on, let's race." Grateful that Mia responded to the challenge, Isabelle summoned her energy and dashed down the length of the paneled line.

"Mia, wait," she called in a loud whisper as her daughter raced around the corner.

"I found the gate, Mama."

Relief turned Isabelle's knees to water as she struggled the remaining distance.

She scanned the metal gate frames, looking for a bell, but

there was nothing. Given how her day was going, that fit perfectly. A hermit probably wouldn't have a bell.

Isabelle raised her fist to knock on the gate just as one of the men rounded the far corner.

She briefly considered running, but there was no way they could continue to outrun him. Terror coursed through her as she saw the other gunman turn the far corner.

With gunmen closing in from both sides, they were out of options.

She quickly pulled Mia into the alcove formed by the frame. Raising her fist, she pounded with all her might. "Help us, please," she screamed. "Open the gate!"

Adam Dalton's head jerked up at sounds from outside. He'd been reading by the fire, his service dog, Chance, resting at his feet when his lights dimmed and a musical chime sounded. Though he'd designed his security system specifically to avoid triggering his PTSD, that particular sequence alerted him to danger. Adrenaline surged through his body and Chance's head lifted as the dog went on full alert.

Adam rested his hand on the Golden Retriever's head, allowing the contact to calm his own racing heart while he opened his tablet and scanned the security app.

Three sides showed nothing, but the view on the fourth side made his breath catch. Someone was pounding on his gate. He zoomed in to see the image more clearly. A woman and a child. He focused his attention and raised the volume until he could make out a faint call for help.

He pressed the button on the intercom. "Do you need something?"

"Let us in, please! Before they kill us."

Sooner than Adam could respond, the sound of gunshots exploded through his speakers.

His heart started to race again and black spots danced in front of his eyes.

Chance leaned into his leg. Adam settled back and ran his hand over the dog's head. The softness of the fur centered him.

He turned to the camera. More gunshots sounded and the woman's pleas were more desperate now.

Although every instinct screamed *hide*, he couldn't ignore her. He took a deep breath and pressed a button. The gate swung inward and he called through the intercom, "Come in."

Caught off balance, the woman fell forward, twisting her body as she hit the ground. She rolled sideways and he caught a glimpse of a bundle wrapped in a blanket. Was she holding a baby?

Shouts and more gunfire drew his attention away from her. He pressed another button and watched anxiously, praying the gates would close in time.

One man managed to angle the tip of his gun just in time to fire a shot before the gate clicked into place locking the men outside. The shot went off to her right, just missing the small child. He had to get down there and help them.

"Chance, come." Adam took the elevator to the ground floor. While it descended, he put a call in to the sheriff, asking his friend to send backup. By the time Adam managed to get to the front door and fling it open, the child and the woman carrying the baby were making their way up the path. He stepped out onto the porch.

It went against his every introverted inclination to invite strangers into his mountain home, but they stood before him, a huddled trio in desperate need of help. The baby was crying, the child looked terrified, and the woman appeared on the verge of collapse. An inner chivalric instinct he'd thought long dead surfaced.

"Come inside. You'll be safe here."

As they stepped up onto the porch, the woman raised shell-shocked eyes. Her expression resonated deep within him. He recognized that state of disbelief where a part of your brain knew you'd experienced something traumatic, but for the most part, you had not begun to process anything beyond the terror.

He ushered them inside and shut the door firmly behind him.

The woman's whole body sagged in relief. "Thank you for letting us in. I don't know what we would have done—"

Another shot sounded from outside, followed by the sound of shattering glass.

She flinched and glanced wildly around. "We have to call the sheriff."

"I already called. He's on his way. In the meantime, you're safe here. They may shoot out a window, but they can't get in."

"You're sure?"

He held up his tablet. "I can monitor from here. See." He held out the device so she could eye the four screens. One of them showed the men pacing outside the fence. "There is no way for them to get over the wall."

She still looked doubtful, but there was nothing more he could do to reassure her until the sheriff arrived. What should he do with them until then? It had been too long since he'd allowed anyone other than his mother and sister inside these walls. He had no idea how to play host.

Adam quietly took in a calming breath and relaxed. He could use his military training and focus on their immediate needs. If he thought of this as a rescue mission rather than as having guests in his home, he could function. The woman was shivering, so the first thing was to warm them up.

"Let's go into the parlor. I'll build a fire so you can dry off."

She came reluctantly, her gaze glancing off the high ceilings and shrouded corridors. Seeing his home through her eyes, he suspected she was wondering if she was heading deeper into danger. He wanted to assure her, but his social skills were too rusty. Words failed him. He hadn't even managed to introduce himself.

He opened the door into a formal room he rarely used. The fireplace was kept ready, though, so he quickly lit the fire and pulled the sofa closer so they could feel the heat. He stood back, letting her unwrap the baby and settle the child beside her.

Next, he needed to gather intel. "Can you tell me what happened? If I update the sheriff, he can send out an alert for the gunmen, so they don't escape. Who are they?"

The woman closed her eyes and drew in a ragged breath. She was still struggling to calm herself. "I don't know."

"It was supposed to be a game, but the bad men chased us with their guns."

Adam glanced over at the child who was peering out from beside the woman. He wanted to pursue the point, but he sensed a need to distract the girl before the woman would speak.

He knelt to be at eye level with the child. "My name is Adam. My dog is good at defeating bad men. Would you like to meet him?" At her shy nod, he signaled Chance. "This is Chance. He's a working dog, so he waited for a command from me, but he's friendly."

The child scooted to the edge of the sofa and held her fingers out for the dog to sniff.

"Would you like to sit and pet him?"

She beamed at him. "May I, Mama?"

How could anyone resist that sweet, imploring look?

Mama didn't. She nodded and Adam was rewarded by a slight easing of the strain on her face. Once he had gotten the child set up on the floor beside Chance, he turned his attention back to the woman.

"Tell me what happened."

She shivered involuntarily. He grabbed a fleece blanket from a pile at the end of the sofa and helped her drape it around her shoulders.

"Thank you." She cradled the baby and huddled into the blanket. "I don't know what to tell the sheriff. I was babysitting for my friend. This is her daughter, Laura. That's Mia— my daughter." The woman nodded toward the older child gently petting Chance.

"She called and told me to take the children and get out of the house. We climbed out the back window as those men broke in through the front door. They started shooting at us. We ran and they chased us through the woods. I saw your gate and started banging." She got the words out in one breath and then shuddered and sank deeper into the blanket.

"Where is your friend?"

Her face fell and he immediately feared the worst.

When she spoke, her soft voice sounded confused, uncertain. "I don't know." She cast a glance at the child and spoke in a low voice. "When she called… I heard gunshots… I don't know."

A tear slid down her face and again Adam was overwhelmed by uncertainty. She was a stranger and a woman, and he had no idea how to comfort her. "I'll call the sheriff again." He glanced down at the child with the dog. "I'll step out into the hallway so she can't hear, but I won't leave you."

"Thank you, Adam."

He'd started for the door but turned back. "I didn't ask your name."

"Isabelle Weaver."

"I'd say pleased to meet you, Isabelle, but under the circumstances…" His voice faded off as she smiled.

Her entire face lit up, the worry fading momentarily, and his heartbeat sped up again. This time Chance didn't help.

He closed the door behind him, but just before it clicked into place, he heard the child's voice.

"He doesn't seem like the billy goat, Mama. He's a nice man."

Warmth spread through his chest. He had no idea what the billy goat reference meant, but it had been a long time since anyone had called him nice.

But nice didn't keep people alive.

TWO

By the time she'd finished recounting the story to Sheriff Nate Brant, all Isabelle wanted to do was to crawl into bed and sleep for a year—an impossible wish with two children to care for and a target on her back.

"I'm sorry we have to impose on you even longer," she apologized as Adam returned from seeing the sheriff out.

He waved off her concern. "Nate was right to have you wait. Let him secure the scene while you stay here, out of danger." Isabelle winced at hearing Jess's house referred to as a crime scene. She'd been trying to stay strong, but just that wording was enough to pierce the numbness and send tears rushing to her eyes.

"Is there anything I can get for you?"

She started to decline, but Mia's head popped up from where she still snuggled with Chance. "I'm hungry, Mama."

"Let me see what I can find to help with that. Chance, stay."

Adam headed off into the dark hallway. When he returned, the delicious aroma reminded Isabelle of how long it had been since they'd eaten.

He set down a tray with soup, crusty bread, and a plate of chicken fingers that made Mia squeal in delight. Isabelle sampled the soup and her taste buds shared Mia's enthusiasm.

"Mmm, this is delicious. You made it?"

He looked up sheepishly. "I heated it. My mother and sister worry about me starving if left to my own devices, so they stock the freezer."

She glanced at the plate of chicken fingers but didn't say anything.

Adam laughed. "Those are all me."

He quickly sobered. "Nate called while I was in the kitchen. He'll be back soon to pick you up. He needs you to look over the house, see if anything is missing."

Other than Jess.

"A bit of good news, though. I checked my security footage. It picked up some pretty clear images of the men—"

The baby wailed, interrupting Adam, and she looked up at him in desperation. "She must be hungry. I don't suppose your mother stocked you with baby food too."

He frowned and shook his head. "No, but I could probably mash some carrots."

For some reason, the image of this tall, rugged man mashing carrots for a baby undid the composure Isabelle had managed to cling to until now. She rose and began to pace the room as the realization of her responsibility for baby Laura settled on her shoulders. Tears pooled in her eyes as she cuddled the infant. *Oh, Jess. What is happening?*

By the time they'd finished eating and feeding Laura, Sheriff Brant arrived to escort her to the crime scene. "We should leave the children here with Adam," he suggested.

"No." Realizing how rude her response had sounded, Isabelle apologized. "I'm sorry. I just—"

Adam stayed her apology with a raised hand. "I understand. You need the children where you can see them. I'll come with you and keep them in the car."

His gentle tone and kind expression nearly undid her again. "Thank you."

They went out and settled the children into a car seat and booster the sheriff pulled from his trunk. At the last minute, Adam ducked back inside. He came out bearing a heavy jacket. "It will be too big, but it's warmer than yours."

Isabelle gratefully accepted the coat and snuggled in its warmth as she climbed into the back seat and instinctively slumped down. Nate had come and gone with no sign of the gunmen, but a wave of anxiety left her feeling vulnerable as they exited the safety of Adam's compound.

The drive down to Jess's house was much faster than her flight through the woods had been. Too fast. Isabelle chewed on her lip to stop herself from begging him to turn around. It would take more strength than she had left to enter that house. She offered a silent plea. *Lord, give me strength.*

The driveway was blocked off with crime scene tape, so Nate pulled up in front of the house. He turned to Isabelle. "We should leave the children here. I can have a deputy stay with them." He glanced at the man beside him. "Or maybe Adam can babysit."

Isabelle's nerves were too on edge to consider leaving the children with a man who was a veritable stranger.

"You can trust him, Ms. Weaver," Nate murmured before adding in a teasing voice, "I'm sure he could handle a baby."

The sheriff's words and tone reassured her. His gentle ribbing tone resonated with the feel of an old friendship. She sent Adam an apologetic smile. "Do you mind?"

"No, go. Do what you need to. Nate's right. A crime scene is no place for children."

Except these children had lived through the crime.

"Thank you. I'll take the baby, though. She's starting to fret, and you've already gone above and beyond today."

The sheriff led the way across the lawn. "I'm avoiding the drive since you said they parked there."

Isabelle stepped over a small mound of snow and stopped to adjust the blanket around Laura. She tugged Adam's coat around her shoulders before starting toward the house again. He had been so generous to them. The thought of his kindness fueled her courage.

As they approached the door, she hesitated again, fussing at the blanket, at the way the folds were twisted.

"Ms. Weaver? It won't be any easier five minutes from now," Nate urged softly.

"Isabelle, please. And I know." She also knew why she was stalling. Walking through that door was tantamount to admitting that Jess was involved in something extremely dangerous.

Stalling wasn't going to change that.

Nate's hand touched her elbow gently. "I'm here with you. The sooner we go in, the faster we can get on with finding your friend."

Isabelle pressed her lips to the baby's soft fluff of hair. "We'll find your mama," she promised and then shoved her shoulders back, lifted her head and faced the sheriff. "Okay. Let's do this."

Despite her resolve, her footsteps faltered as she stepped through the doorway. Nate had said the house had been tossed, but that word hadn't prepared her for the chaos.

Her eyes watered as she took in the scene. Memories of Christmas morning flooded her mind. A week ago, she and Mia had spent the night so the girls could share Laura's first Christmas morning. Now the tree had been destroyed, flipped on its side, and ornaments littered the ground. What had they hoped to find by doing that? It just seemed malicious, and that ratcheted her fears.

She turned her gaze to the kitchen where she and Jess had teamed up with Mia to make Christmas pancakes. Just hours ago, she'd stood at that same stove warming Laura's bottle.

Her purse and car keys still sat on the counter, but absolutely everything else was chaos. She pushed back the horror of the scene and tried to study the room.

"Someone was angry." It seemed such an understatement, but Nate had asked for her impressions.

"Why do you say that?"

"Because there's the obvious evidence of a search—the drawers pulled open, the sofa slit, the closet door ajar and the contents strewn around." She shuddered thinking that the men who had done this were the same ones who had chased her into the woods. If Adam hadn't let them in… Tremors started and her whole body began to shake violently.

"Isabelle, I'm here. You're safe."

The feel of the sheriff's hand on her shoulder tethered her, and slowly the tremors subsided. She shook off the thoughts and circled the room, focusing on what lay before her.

"They were looking for something, but there's more, a second layer of violence that scares me on a deeper level. Because who destroys a Christmas tree when they're looking for people? Who rips stockings from the mantel?"

Nate nodded. "Very perceptive. But you have no idea what they were looking for?"

"Besides us? No."

She ran Jess's words through her head again. "When Jess called, she told me to get out of the house. She didn't indicate there was anything here I should take besides her daughter."

The sheriff came to stand beside her so they could take in the room from the same perspective. "I want you to think outside the box for a minute. Could Jess have done this? Could she have been with the men?"

The idea filled Isabelle with such hope that, for the first time, she realized how terrified she was that her friend had not survived.

"No, this wouldn't have been Jess looking for anything. She wouldn't have had to toss her own house. She'd have known what she'd wanted."

"Unless she wanted it to look like she didn't know."

Isabelle stopped her visual search of the room and turned to face the sheriff. "What are you implying?"

He held up his hands in surrender at her accusatory tone. "I wasn't implying anything."

"But you're thinking something."

"You're a mind reader?"

"I'm a mother. I know when someone is being evasive."

He gave a chuckle. "Okay. Well, I'm keeping an open mind, but based on what you've told me and the evidence at this crime scene—and the lack of it—there are several possibilities."

"And they are?"

"I'm holding them close to my vest at the moment, so I can keep that open mind."

Isabelle had to respect his investigative process, but that didn't stop her from forming her own conclusions.

"This is what I'm thinking. One." She ticked the number off on her finger. "The men came back here and searched the house—which they could have done quickly because it isn't very big. They were angry that the children and I got away and took it out here.

"Or two." She ticked another finger. "They had Jess with them and were trying to get her to deliver something. When she didn't, they destroyed her home."

He nodded, and her heart sank. She really didn't want it to be true. Because that didn't bode well for Jess.

"Or, three. They left, and Jess came back on her own before you got here."

The sheriff shrugged. "All three are possible, but I'm not

jumping at anything until the crime scene team is done and I see what they've got."

Isabelle had to accept that. "If we're done, may I go look for my phone?"

"Sorry, no. But I'll ask the deputies to keep an eye out."

She understood. They couldn't have her tramping through a crime scene. "Am I allowed to take baby supplies?"

"I'd prefer we not disturb anything. With all this mess, anything we change could alter the evidence. When we catch these guys, and we will, I don't want anything interfering with their prosecution."

Isabelle nodded. "Got it. I have some supplies for her at my house." She sighed as fatigue washed over her. "May I go home now?"

"I'll have to find someone to drive you."

"It's okay. Besides Mia's booster seat, I have another seat for Laura in my car. It's parked out front."

"With all the tires slashed."

Isabelle closed her eyes and sagged against the wall.

"I'm sorry, Isabelle. Damaging your car must make it feel more personal."

She heaved a sigh. "It became personal when they started shooting at me."

Once Isabelle had gone into the house, Adam had let Chance settle on the back seat. As he glanced at his dog tucked against Mia. Adam wondered for the umpteenth time how he'd managed to get himself caught up in this. To be fair, they'd come to his gate, and it would have taken a man with a far colder heart than his to turn away a woman and children in such desperate straits. He couldn't live with the guilt if they came to harm. After his years in Afghanistan, too many deaths already weighed on his conscience.

But knowing it was the right thing to do wasn't the same as being comfortable. Truthfully, this was the most human interaction he'd had in five years. Pretty much the only real interaction he'd had with anyone other than his mother and sister. And Nate. He and the sheriff had served three tours together, and Nate was possibly the only living person who truly understood what Adam had endured. Sometimes he wondered if he would even have survived were it not for Nate's persistent friendship.

The sound of the front door closing interrupted his musings, and Adam looked up to see Isabelle and Nate walking down the path. His heart went out to the woman trudging over the snowy lawn. There was another answer for why he'd had to help. Regardless of the personal cost, how could he turn his back on someone who was so bravely coping with this difficult situation?

She snuggled the baby close, but there was a new weariness to her and she looked even more frail than she had earlier. Nate walked beside her with his phone to his ear. Adam could tell from his posture and facial expression that it was not good news. The sheriff disconnected the call as they approached the car, and from the set of his jaw, Adam got an uneasy sense that his involvement wasn't over. "Back to the floor, Chance."

Nate held the back door open to help Isabelle into the vehicle. He came around, got in the driver's side, and turned to Adam, his expression sober.

"There's been a bad accident up on the ridge. I need to head up to the site, but I can't leave this crime scene unattended. If I leave the deputy here, will you take Isabelle home?"

Isabelle spoke up before Adam could reply. "Again, I'm sorry to be so much trouble. Apparently, they slashed my tires, but I can wait here for someone to come back. You've already done far more for us than necessary. I couldn't possibly ask you to help again."

"It would be better for Adam to take you."

Adam read the subtext in Nate's blunt statement. Whatever he'd seen inside had made the sheriff wary of Isabelle leaving on her own. Questions rose in his mind. Did his friend think Isabelle was at risk? Or did he suspect her?

The sheriff cleared his throat. "I'm sorry, Isabelle. Until we know who they are and what they want, we really don't know how safe you are anywhere."

And just like that, Adam found himself agreeing to help. There was something about this woman that slipped beneath his wall of reserve and undid his reclusive instincts. He turned in his seat to reassure her. "You didn't ask. Nate did. And he's right. You've had a rough day. Let me take you home."

All the fight seemed to leave her at his offer. Emotion flitted across her face. Relief welled in her eyes. She bowed her head for a moment before lifting her head to him and nodding. "Thank you."

The sheriff made quick work of retrieving Mia's booster and the spare car seat from Isabelle's car before he drove them back to Adam's house. After leaving the seats on the ground by the open garage, and promising to update them when he knew anything, Nate took off.

Adam watched the taillights disappear down the lane as Nate's words echoed in his brain. *We really don't know how safe you are anywhere.* Panic clawed at his throat. He was now solely responsible for safeguarding a frightened woman and two innocent children. He should never have accepted responsibility. He should have volunteered to stay at the crime scene and let the deputy take them home. He wasn't enough to protect them, he—

The solid bulk of Chance leaning into his legs cut off the

panicked thoughts before they could overwhelm him. Adam ruffled his hand through the dog's fur. He took a deep breath and cleared his throat. "Let me just get these seats in the car and we can head to your house."

Isabelle angled her head and offered a tentative smile. "Have you installed one of these recently? The directions are ridiculously complicated, but I've done it enough times that it's second nature. Why don't you take the baby while I set up the car seats?" Isabelle held Laura toward him.

Left with no choice, Adam accepted the baby, who started to squawk as he shifted her awkwardly, trying to find a good hold. Isabelle laughed and, for a moment, his heart stilled at the unexpectedly joyful sound.

"She's not a bomb," Isabelle joked then looked thoughtful as Laura continued to cry. "Did you ever play football?"

Adam nodded.

"There's something called a football hold. Babies love it. Just cradle her the way you would a football while running for a touchdown."

Adam shifted the baby as directed, and her cries instantly turned to happy gurgles. Amazed, he rocked her gently while Isabelle installed the car seat and got Mia perched in her booster seat.

Once everyone was settled and Isabelle's address was programmed into his GPS, Adam started the car down the driveway. The soft snow from earlier had turned to sleet, and he wanted to get her home quickly. "Do you have supplies for the baby at your house, or should we stop somewhere?"

"I have enough to get through the night." A heavy silence hung in the air for a few minutes before Isabelle spoke again, her voice low, presumably to keep her daughter from hearing.

"About what Nate said…."

Adam heard the tremor in her voice and wished there was something he could say to set her fears to rest.

"Do you think he's serious? I mean not serious but…right? About the danger."

Adam debated how to answer. He could give her the truth—that Nate would not have said anything without a reasonably strong belief he was right. Or he could play it more gently and say the sheriff was just taking precautions. But if he downplayed it and something happened to her or the girls, then it would be on him.

He shrugged. "I don't know, Isabelle. I can only say I've never known Nate to be an alarmist. If he thinks your safety is at risk, we should be careful."

Adam heard her swallow. A quick sideways glance showed her fighting back tears. Adam wanted to reach across and take her hand, comfort her. But what comfort did he have to offer really? Except… "We should pray."

Isabelle looked surprised at his response.

He shrugged. "It's what I do when I don't know what else to do. I remind myself that God is in control." The words sounded so simple spilling from his lips. They gave no indication of the hard-fought battle it had taken him to get to this place of trust in God. An ongoing battle, like so much of his recovery.

"Mama taught me to say 'Jesus, I trust in you.'"

Adam smiled into his rearview mirror. "That's an excellent prayer, Mia."

Isabelle nodded, so he focused his gaze on the road that was icing over and whispered the words he could hear Isabelle praying with her daughter. "Jesus, I trust in you."

The words settled a calmness over the car that lasted until he made the turn onto Isabelle's street.

"Which house is yours?"

She didn't answer right away. "Isabelle?"

"The one with a car in the driveway." The tremor was back in her voice, alerting him.

"Not your second car?" He realized in that moment that he knew nothing about her. Did she have a husband who was waiting for her? The thought bothered him more than it should.

"Not mine."

Adam slowed as they pulled closer.

"Adam, wait. That's the car the men were driving."

"The gunmen?"

She could barely get the words out. "I think. Yes. It's the same make and color as the car that was at Jess's house."

"Okay, don't panic." The command was as much for himself as it was for her. "They won't know my car. Just don't look over that way as we drive by. We'll just keep driving down the street."

"It's a dead end."

Adam blew out a breath. This just got better and better. "How many other houses are there?"

"Five and a cul-de-sac."

He thought for a minute. "Here's the plan. You slide down in the seat, so they don't see you. I'm going to drive down the road and circle back. If anyone is watching, hopefully they'll think I dropped you off back there."

"Or you could really drop me off. There's a path through the woods. It comes out the other side."

"No. If you had a cell phone, I'd consider it, but it's too dangerous to separate with no way to communicate. Is the path wide enough to drive down?"

"It's barely wide enough for a stroller."

Scratch that idea. If he'd had the truck, he might try it, but not with the SUV.

Adam glanced over at the house as he drove by. He could see lights on and silhouettes of men moving around inside.

"Take my phone and call the sheriff. Tell him about the car and that there are two men inside." Her soft whimper made his heart ache, but she dutifully took the phone and made the call as he circled around the cul-de-sac and headed back.

"There's someone on the stoop now, so stay down. I'll let you know when we're past. Hopefully, they'll just think I made a wrong turn."

The first bullet slamming against his windshield put paid to that notion.

"New plan. Hang on!"

THREE

Adam sped to the corner and made a sharp right. Isabelle held her breath as the car skidded on the icy road. She wanted to beg him to slow down, but men firing bullets was an even more deadly threat than the icy roads. She glanced at the children in the back seat and whispered another prayer. *Lord, please help us.*

"Talk to me, Isabelle. I don't want to get trapped in another dead end. What do I need to know about these streets?"

Isabelle pushed back at the terror that was threatening to overwhelm her. She knew this neighborhood. She just had to think clearly to figure it out. "These streets are all dead ends, but take the next one down, right after this curve. There's a house at the end with a driveway that goes through to the next block."

"That will do." Adam flew around the curve then slammed on the brake as he headed into the hard turn. The car fishtailed again, but he quickly corrected and raced down the dark street.

Isabelle clung to the safety handle and continued to pray. They were traveling far faster than she'd like on a residential street with lights few and far between. "Could we pull into a driveway, turn off the lights and wait?"

"Too late," Adam muttered as a pair of headlights swung around the corner behind him, eliminating that option.

She fought against the fear threatening to paralyze her. "The road curves up ahead. The house with the driveway is the last one on the left. If we can get far enough ahead, they might not see us. The driveway is long and goes behind the house. Usually there are no cars outside, but sometimes they park near the garage. The garage opens on both sides, but there's also a paved area beside it. If you drive around it, you'll come out the other side and onto the street."

Adam didn't ease up on the gas until he swung into the driveway.

Isabelle gave a soft cry of disbelief as the car's headlights lit up the driveway—and the solid wall of snow that blocked their path. "Oh no!"

Her gaze flew from the blocked drive to Adam's face. His expression was grim, his jaw set. Guilt for involving him flooded her. "I'm sorry."

"Don't worry. I have a plan."

He had a plan? How could he have come up with something so quickly. Her brain had barely had time to register the danger, but he was already swinging the car in a circle. He pulled all the way to the end of the drive, against a huge snow drift.

"Maybe they won't see us?"

He chuffed a sound somewhere between a chuckle and a grunt. "Maybe. But I'm not banking on it." He lowered his voice, but the tone was urgent. "I need you to open the glove compartment and hand me the gun."

Gun. Shivers raced through Isabelle. What did he have in mind?

"Isabelle. Now."

The urgency in his voice jolted her out of her shock. Her trembling fingers fumbled with the latch, but finally she got it open and reached in for the handgun. Her brain couldn't wrap itself around the idea that she was in a car with the children, with men after them, and she was holding a gun. She passed it to Adam with lightning speed and turned, hoping to see the children asleep. Mia stared back, her eyes wide with terror, and Isabelle's heart cracked a little more.

Adam rolled his window down and a chill wind blew through the car. Laura started to whimper. "Do I have time to climb back there with them?"

"No. I need you to get down below window level, but stay belted in."

Tremors shook her body, a combination of fear and the cold. Why hadn't she ridden back there? She should be there to protect her babies. "Mia, stay as low as you can."

A squeal of tires alerted her that the other vehicle had caught up. *Please, God, let Adam's plan, whatever it is, work.* She huddled in her seat, watching him as she repeated her prayer in a litany. He was so still. She could feel the icy tension radiating off him, but he sat calmly, gun resting on the window frame, waiting.

Laura's whimpers rose to a cry and Isabelle prayed she couldn't be heard over the sound of the engine. "Shh, baby, it will be all right."

The next few moments passed in a blur of sound and motion, gunshots, tires squealing, metal scraping. And then Adam was gunning the engine and she felt the car take flight. Mia screamed, Laura's wails rose to a crescendo, but Adam remained calm. "You can sit up now, but keep your seat belt tight."

"What?" Still in a state of shock, Isabelle listened to him speak to her daughter. His voice was gentle, but it had a detached quality to it that sent chills down her spine. She glanced at his white-knuckled grip on the wheel, and suspicions grew.

"Mia, I'm sorry if that scared you. Everything is fine now. I only shot out their tire so they can't chase us anymore."

"Thank you, Mr. Adam."

Isabelle's heart swelled, overwhelmed with gratitude for this man who not only protected them, but who took the time to reassure an anxious child. As she turned to thank him, she could see the tension still etched in his neck and shoulders, the jaw so firmly set it looked frozen in place. Dread overcame her already shattered nerves. She knew that look. She knew the signs of a man gripped in memories of war. A new kind of fear settled over her, one that twisted a knot in her stomach— and had nothing to do with the men who'd been chasing them.

Adam entered the living room, taking in the sight of Mia asleep, snuggled against Chance. She seemed so peaceful. Unlike Isabelle, who was pacing the room with a fretful Laura on her shoulder.

"Any updates?" she asked as he knelt to add a log to the fire.

"I spoke with Nate. He didn't have anything to report except it seems the accident may have been a decoy to draw him away from the crime scene."

Isabelle gave a little shiver, making Adam wish he'd had better news. She continued to pace with the baby for a few minutes before perching on the edge of the sofa.

"Did he describe the car?"

"No. Why?"

"I've been worried the accident involved Jess."

At least he could reassure her on that score. "No, I asked. Nate said the plates were not registered to her."

Isabelle released a soft sigh and settled back into the sofa. "I've been so worried. I didn't even properly thank you for all of this." She gestured to the remains of the meal he'd laid out. "And for stopping for diapers and formula." She smiled softly. "And crayons. You won Mia as a friend for life with those."

She closed her eyes for a moment, taking a deep breath

before she opened them to smile solemnly at him. "You were our hero today, Adam. I can't thank you enough."

Uncomfortable with the praise, Adam shrugged and tried to brush it off. "Crayons and diapers do not a hero make."

"Maybe not, but it was clever of you to suggest she draw what scared her."

He avoided the questioning look in her eyes, the one that wanted to ask how he knew about art therapy. "Why don't you try to get some rest? We don't know what tomorrow will bring, and you must be exhausted."

A shiver ran through her. "I've tried. But every time I close my eyes, I relive it. If you hadn't let us in, I don't know—"

"Breathe, Isabelle."

She did as directed, taking several gulping breaths before she managed to smooth them into a regular pattern. "Will you talk to me? About other things. Happy things. Tell me about your life here."

A chuckle rolled through his chest. Happiness and his life did not exactly go hand in hand. But he understood her need to talk, to fill the silence and turn off the brain.

"There's not much to say about my life. I create adaptive technology."

Isabelle shifted the baby so that Laura was cradled in her arms. "What does that mean?"

Adam laughed. "It's a fancy name for an age-old job. I tinker with things, try to find ways to make them accessible to people with different needs."

"Like these lights?"

Adam was impressed. "What did you notice?"

"There's something different about them. A softness, a tint. They don't feel as overwhelming."

"Very perceptive. My mother gets migraines. This diffused and tinted lighting is less offensive." His mother wasn't the only one who benefitted from the lights, but he had no plan to discuss his brain injury or PTSD with a woman he'd just met, no matter the circumstances.

"That's so clever of you. Did you always…what did you call it? Tinker?"

"My father had a workshop. He was always playing around with designs. I guess I came by it naturally." And relied on it for survival after his injury.

"Tell me about some of your other designs."

Adam spoke softly, hoping the gentle rhythm of his voice would lull her to sleep. Within minutes, he was rewarded as her eyes drifted closed and her head lolled back against the sofa.

At least one of them could relax.

He rose and gently eased Laura from Isabelle's arms. The baby nestled sweetly against his chest as he stood there, trying to absorb the tranquility of the scene. If one didn't know the background, and what had brought Isabelle and the girls to his door, it would be easy to believe this was a quiet family evening.

Something caught in his throat at the thought. *Careful there, Adam*, he admonished himself. It would be too easy to let down his guard and start wanting things he couldn't have, because this was just the sort of idyllic family life he'd once dreamed of having—before war had stolen all his hope.

Frustrated and angry with himself for falling prey to false illusions, Adam settled Laura into a bed of blankets and strode to the window overlooking his yard. He forced himself to take the deep breaths he'd just recommended to Isabelle. What he really needed, though, was to be outside in the woods, with the wind in his face, breathing the fresh pine scent of the trees, feeling the musty earth beneath his feet. Nature had given him the closest thing possible to a cure for his brain injury and PTSD. It had pulled him in and centered him, but tonight, the forest didn't offer the haven he'd come to rely on.

Below him, bright lights from the wall gave the illusion of safety and adequate security, but he knew from harsh experience that deadly dangers could lurk in the impenetrable dark beyond that perimeter.

As he revisited the day, and all the ways it could have gone worse, the spotlights flashed in his eyes, triggering his brain. Darkness began to close in, forming a tunnel as the light grew fainter and smaller. His body tensed as he peered down the tunnel. He couldn't see the enemy, but he knew they were out there. Ready. Waiting.

His chest tightened, his breaths coming in short uneven gasps. He couldn't control the rush of adrenaline, the need to lash out at a force he couldn't see.

A weight pressed insistently against his leg. He tried to shove it away and his hand settled in soft fur. Even then, he tried to push back, but the furry creature was insistent, head butting him and knocking him slightly off balance. That motion interrupted the panic and, as he threaded his hands through Chance's soft fur, the darkness slowly began to recede. Lights glimmered softly in his field of vision.

He took several deep inhales and felt his chest ease, his heart rate become more regulated. He closed his eyes and offered a prayer of gratitude. *You are my strength, Lord. Yours is the glory. Yours is the power.* He ruffled Chance's fur, more lightly this time. "Thanks to you too, buddy."

Isabelle woke feeling stiff and disoriented. She blinked, looking around the room. When she saw Mia asleep by the fire, everything came rushing back at her. Jess's call. The escape through the woods. Adam letting them in. The crime scene and car chase. Talking with Adam.

She must have fallen asleep, like Mia had.

Realizing it was Chance easing away from Mia that had woken her, she turned her head to see where he'd gone. Her breath caught in her throat at the sight of Adam in the grip of a panic attack. *No. No. No.* Fear and regret washed over her. Fear because she knew this too well. Her husband had suffered PTSD. She'd lived with the fallout from it—his savage temper, his flashbacks, the way he'd court danger rather than accept help. She'd been on the verge of leaving him for her daughter's sake when he'd been killed in that last risky mission.

Now she and Mia were dependent on another man who suffered the same way. And that brought on regret, because suddenly everything that had puzzled her made sense—his rusty manners, the isolation of his life, his very home. It didn't take superpowers to understand he'd basically built himself a sanctuary inside a stockade fence.

And she'd invaded it.

Guilt swamped her. She'd sought refuge from him, brought danger into his life again, and unknowingly triggered these attacks. She hadn't been mistaken in the car. He'd fought off an attack then by going into warrior mode. Just like her husband had.

But Adam had Chance. Even as she watched, she could see the dog break the cycle. The tension in Adam's posture relaxed. And that eased something in her heart. Adam was not Daniel. He'd been nothing but kind to her and deserved kindness in return.

She might have invaded his world and brought danger to his sanctuary, but she had also been trained to help someone with PTSD.

She rose and started walking slowly toward him, speaking softly as she approached. "Thank you, Adam, for everything you did for us today." She paused when she was an arm's length away, knowing not to invade his personal space without invitation. "I'm sorry we brought this into your life. You didn't ask for it, but you opened your home to us and provided safety. You protected two innocent children and a terrified woman. I'm so grateful to you for not turning us away. Instead—"

"How did you know?"

Isabelle hesitated only a minute. "That you're a protector? It was evident in every action you took today. You put your own well-being at risk for us—to protect us."

As she kept talking, she noticed his grip on Chance loosen. His shoulders relaxed. He stood silently for a moment. "You recognized what just happened. How did you know?"

She didn't pretend to misunderstand. "My husband completed four tours in Afghanistan. Each one aggravated his PTSD a little more."

"And?"

Her head dropped. "He didn't come home from the fifth deployment."

"I'm sorry."

She cleared her throat. "Thank you."

He turned back to look out the window. "When?"

"Three years ago."

"Mia?"

"She was very young, and he was gone most of the time. And when he was there—well, he was never really there."

Silence fell between them and Isabelle searched for some normal conversation to fill it. "Thank you again for thinking to get the crayons for her. She loves to draw."

He chuckled. "I noticed."

Isabelle glanced at the drawings scattered across the coffee table.

"I meant what I said. You've been amazing to us. So welcoming when I know this must be hard for you."

He shrugged and continued to stare out into the yard.

She could see his reflection in the window and noted the tension building again. Had she said something wrong?

Suddenly, he backed away from the window and turned to face her.

"They've breached the perimeter."

She looked at him in disbelief. "That sounds like a line from a bad movie."

"I'm serious. We have to leave—now."

"I thought you said your security was excellent."

"It is. And they've breached it. Which means they're not your average criminals and we have to get out of here fast. Gather whatever you can grab in two minutes."

While Isabelle picked up the baby, Adam lifted a sleepy Mia. "No need to wake up, sleepyhead, we're just going for a ride."

"Mama?"

"She's right here with Laura."

Mia glanced over, smiled at her mother, and snuggled back into Adam's arms. "And Chance?"

"Leading the way."

Isabelle watched Adam reach down to grab the crayons and pad of paper, and her heart melted despite her fear. She snatched up the diaper bag and followed him through the doorway.

"We'll take the elevator down."

Isabelle heard the tension in his voice despite his matter-of-fact tone. When the elevator opened, she realized they were on an entirely different level from where they'd entered earlier. There was no time for questions as Adam led her to a Range Rover. She should have been surprised to see he'd transferred the car seats earlier, but she was learning not to be surprised by how prepared he was.

They rapidly settled the girls into their seats. Isabelle wanted to stay in the back with them but remembered Adam needing her help earlier. She kissed each girl on the forehead and then reluctantly closed the door and climbed into the front seat.

As soon as she was belted in, Adam powered the engine on and pressed a button that opened a door in the back wall. "This driveway takes us out a different way. It will buy us some time."

Isabelle watched him in confused wonder. The man who, minutes earlier, had been in the grip of a panic attack was now a warrior, laser-focused on keeping them alive. Despite her regret for bringing triggers into his life, she breathed a prayer of thanks to the Lord for directing her to Adam's home.

They sped down a narrow side drive and stopped when they reached the intersection where it met the main road. Adam checked both directions before turning right.

"We're not heading into town?"

"No. Presumably that's what they will expect."

Isabelle shuddered in fear at the idea of these unknown criminals out there anticipating her next move. It seemed second nature to Adam, and she wasn't certain if that reassured or frightened her more.

They drove in silence for only a few minutes before headlights lit up the road from behind, illuminating a heavy truck bearing down on them.

"Brace yourself," Adam muttered as the truck bumped them from behind. A popping sound and whoosh was all the warning they had before something flew by the car and exploded, filling the road ahead with dense red smoke.

Isabelle could barely breathe through her terror as she turned to check on the children. "Adam, what is that?"

"A smoke grenade."

The danger of her earlier flight through the woods paled compared to this new terror.

Adam sped up, putting distance between them and the truck, but the wall of red smoke rapidly expanded, covering the entire road. Isabelle couldn't see a thing as Adam drove through the crimson cloud. Then she felt the car jolt as he suddenly swerved off the road.

Pine tree branches smacked against the windshield.

Isabelle screamed and covered her eyes as the forest closed in around them.

FOUR

Isabelle's scream echoed through the vehicle as the SUV careened through the dark forest like a runaway train, taking out branches as it continued down the mountain. How had it come to this? Who were these men and why did they want to kill her?

"Isabelle, it's okay." Adam's voice broke through her terrified thoughts.

Nothing is okay, she wanted to cry. *Someone is trying to kill me and these babies, and I have no idea why.*

His voice persisted. "See that safety hold in the roof? Grab on to it. The ride will be rough, but we're not crashing."

"You're sure?" Peering at him through her clasped fingers, she could see his profile outlined by the light from the dash and thought she saw the hint of a smile despite the grim circumstances.

"I am."

"But the girls—"

"Will be fine. Their car seats are secure."

Isabelle turned to check for herself. Mia's eyes were wide and Laura was whining, but they looked physically fine.

"Let me guess. You have a plan?"

He did laugh at that. But he never took his eyes off the road. "I do."

Road. She let the word register. They were now back on

an actual road, not plunging off the side of a cliff. Now that she could breathe, Isabelle took a moment to study the snow-packed dirt illuminated by his low-beam headlights. Calling it a road might be generous. It was more a rough worn track lined by towering pine trees. "What is this?"

"An old logging trail. It runs parallel to the road—more or less. But hang on tight. It wasn't built for full-size cars."

Isabelle was grateful for the warning as the SUV seemed to suddenly plunge again. The screech died in her throat this time, but she didn't let go of her grip.

Despite Adam's calm words, the sight outside her windows was terrifying. His choice of vehicle made sense now. They seemed to be driving straight into a forest, and no ordinary car would have been able to push through the branches that hung low over them and scratched the roof. It was like being in a carwash when those big rollers came at you. Maybe she could ease Mia's fear by describing it that way.

She glanced over her shoulder, ready to reassure her daughter, but the sight that met her eyes stole her words. Mia was leaning over from her booster seat, trying to comfort Laura. The soft sound of her daughter singing a lullaby flooded Isabelle with love and pride. In all honesty, she was a little in awe of her own daughter and her fierce love for Jess's little girl.

"She's just like you."

Adam's gentle words surprised her. "Apparently, she's braver than I am. I didn't hear her screaming." Now that they had escaped the imminent threat to their lives, shame at her reaction flooded her.

"Isabelle, cut yourself some slack. It's been a very long day. You have nothing to be embarrassed about. I think you've been amazing."

A flush of another kind suffused her. "I've only done what

I had to." She hesitated a moment then lowered her voice. "I'm so sorry I dragged you into this. I shouldn't have—"

"Shouldn't have what? Banged on my gate to save the children's lives? Shouldn't have run from men trying to kill you? Isabelle, you have done absolutely everything right today. You've been as brave as any soldier I ever fought with."

"Until I screamed like a baby."

He laughed again, and the sound of it warmed her heart.

"Thank you, Adam. You've been pretty amazing yourself."

"There you go. We're a good team. We just—"

His words were cut off by the sound of rapid fire from above. Bullets hammered the door of the SUV. The driver's-side window was hit and spider-webbed. "Get down"

Adam killed the headlights and threw a cloth over the dashboard. They were instantly enveloped in a darkness so deep that Isabelle couldn't see an inch in front of her. "Mia?" Panic washed over her at the thought of the babies being hit by that barrage.

"I'm okay, Mama."

"Adam?"

"Fine. Remember how I told you the road ran parallel to us?"

Isabelle squeaked out a yes.

"That's the bad news. Apparently, they know it too. But there is good news. They can shoot from up there, but they can't get down here unless they go get a smaller vehicle and follow."

"They can't climb down?"

"No, it's a sheer drop-off from the road. They could come in on foot, but we have too much of a head start."

Adam had slowed the Rover to a crawl. How could he even see where he was going? "What do we do now if we can't use the lights to see the way?"

He let out a deep sigh. "I'm going to need your help."

Isabelle closed her eyes and prayed. "Okay. What do I have to do?"

"I want you to open your door a crack—just enough that you can see the edge of the road. I'll keep driving, but you have to make sure I stay on the road. I would do it from my side, but my door's jammed—the bullets must've hit the locking mechanism."

"I can do that. But won't they hear the engine?"

"It has a special insulation that makes it more like a soft purr, but we're not going to stay in it much longer anyway. Mia?"

"Yes, Mr. Adam."

"I loved listening to your singing, but with the door open we have to be very quiet now, okay?"

"Okay."

Adam's voice had dropped to a whisper. Heavy silence fell over the SUV, silence that pulsed with tension and the absence of a sweet lullaby. Isabelle rubbed her eyes, praying that she would wake up and find this nightmare was over.

"Why do you think they stopped shooting?"

"I don't know."

That didn't reassure her. "Is it too much to hope they got tired and went home?"

He chuckled softly. "We can hope…but let's keep moving. Whenever you're ready."

Isabelle eased the door open and was immediately hit by a shower of ice pellets. She shrugged them off, just grateful they weren't bullets. Following Adam's lead, she whispered, "We're about a foot from the edge."

The SUV eased forward. "Let me know if I get closer than six inches."

Muscles strained against the tension in Isabelle's arms as she tried to hold the door open against the impact of icy-coated tree branches. The wind was picking up, whistling through the gap hauntingly. Isabelle shivered but kept her gaze glued to the snow-dirt mix as she clung to the door with all her might. "So far, so good. Totally straight."

Inch by inch, the Range Rover crept along in the dark with only the occasional hint of moonlight through the trees to guide them.

"Oh, you're getting too close." Isabelle's eyes were glazing over and she'd nearly missed the way the SUV was drifting toward the roadside. She couldn't see beyond the dirt ridge, but she was pretty sure she didn't want to know how sharply it dropped off.

Adam adjusted, and they were headed straight again. Time slowed into a monotonous crawl along the edge of the trees. The snow had ended, and moonlight peeped from beneath the clearing clouds.

"We're here," Adam finally whispered.

Isabelle peered into the darkness but, despite the moonlight, she couldn't see anything other than trees behind more trees. "Where is here?"

"Well, this is stop one. We ditch the car here."

Isabelle didn't even want to ask what came next. Ditching the car sounded too much like it involved walking, and she was beyond exhausted. "We can't stay here for the night?"

"Not unless you want to freeze to death."

Before she could breathe a word of assent, Adam turned the wheel sharply.

"Adam, you're off the path."

"I know."

What was he doing? She pulled the door closed and sank into her seat, raising her arms protectively as the SUV drove straight into a wall of trees before coming to a stop in a clearing.

"Wait here," he murmured. "I need to camouflage the car. Then I'll come back for you. It's only a short hike to the cabin."

Isabelle simply nodded. Exhaustion kept her silent as Adam walked away from the SUV.

Adam knew he was pushing Isabelle and the children beyond their physical limits, but he had no choice if they wanted to live. While he layered the SUV in pine branches and scattered leaves and snow, his brain calculated the best way to transition to his cabin. He wove the last set of branches in place, satisfied his camouflage would hide their trail—at least for the night.

He opened the driver's-side door and stuck his head in. "Stay here for a few minutes. I just want to scout and make sure we've left them far behind." What he didn't tell her was that if they hadn't lost the men, they were in deeper trouble than he wanted to consider. His hiking cabin would give them shelter, but it had no defense capability.

Adam crept back along the trail, sticking to the tree line and pausing every few steps to listen. The forest was full of the sound of branches crackling as the wind put pressure on the snow-laden boughs. He stood. Silent. Eyes closed. Making himself insignificant... almost invisible—a technique he'd first learned in the army and perfected in his forest therapy classes—until he felt one with the natural world around him. He could hear an owl hoot in the distance, but it was a calm and normal sound, not alarmed by an intruder. No other animals gave any indication of disturbance. High above, on the roadway, he could hear the regular passing of traffic, but deep within the woods, peace reigned. Slowly exhaling his relief, he opened his eyes and headed back to his SUV.

Isabelle had fallen asleep in the front seat and the girls were both asleep in the back. Peace reigned in here, as well, and after the day they'd been through, he hated to wake them. But he had no choice. The temperature was sinking fast and running the engine for heat would defeat the point of camouflage.

Adam eased into his seat and leaned toward her. "Isabelle," he whispered.

She woke in a flash, reflexively raising her arms in a defensive move. "Isabelle, it's me, Adam. It's all clear. We can head to the cabin." He kept his voice low, his arms resting limply in his lap, so she wouldn't feel threatened as she came fully alert.

She blinked, confusion evident on her face. Adam fought the urge to comfort her. Something about Isabelle called to his protective instincts. In her sleepy state, she looked so vulnerable. He dragged his thoughts back to the task at hand: getting them to the cabin safely, keeping them alive.

"I was going to carry Mia piggyback and hold Laura, but Mia's sleepy and I don't want her to fall. If I carry her, can you manage the baby?"

Isabelle nodded and a resolute expression settled on her face. "I will."

"Okay, it should only take us about twenty minutes to get there."

Her eyes widened, but that was the only sign of distress she showed.

"Is it safe to get out now?"

"Yes. I tracked back far enough to be sure they haven't followed."

He noted the wary relief on her face, his words seemingly having given her a new energy. She opened Mia's side of the car and climbed in beside her daughter. Adam knew he should afford her some privacy, but he couldn't force himself to avert his eyes. There was something in her gentle touch, the soft whisper of her voice waking Mia, that inspired him.

"Mr. Adam is going to carry you on a new adventure. Are you ready?"

The soft-spoken words drifted to him. He could barely make out Mia's sleepy response, but Isabelle backed out of the vehicle and guided the little girl to him.

"Hey, sleepyhead," he teased. "Ready to find the enchanted cabin in the forest?" He was rewarded with a gleam of excitement in her eyes.

While he got a blanket to wrap around Mia, Isabelle lifted Laura from her car seat and snuggled the baby deep within her coat. Adam grabbed the diaper bag and they headed deeper into the forest.

Moonlight filtered gently through the clouds. He stepped up beside Isabelle. "There is no sign of the men, but humans aren't the only dangers in this forest. Walk carefully, stay on the snow as much as possible, and try not to make a sound."

Her wide-eyed look of terror drove a knife through his heart. He reached for her arm. "Trust me. Do as I say and we'll be fine."

FIVE

Isabelle yawned, stretched, and looked around the small room where she'd slept with the girls. Last night she'd been nearly comatose by the time they'd dragged themselves inside, so she hadn't taken time to observe more than the beds. She glanced over at the two sleeping children. It hadn't taken much to get them settled in. Once the novelty of being in a cabin in the woods had worn off, Mia had curled up beside Chance and immediately fallen into a deep sleep. Sometime during the night, the dog had slipped away, but Mia still slept. Laura had fretted a bit, but a change of diaper and a bottle had settled her too. Isabelle had crashed not long after. It was both a testament to her trust in Adam and a sign of the depth of her exhaustion—mental and physical—that she'd slept so soundly.

The aroma of fresh coffee pulled her from the cozy nest of blankets. She shivered as she stood, so she pulled another blanket over Mia and grabbed one to wrap around herself. Still tired, she stumbled out of the bedroom in search of Adam.

As she studied the dwelling through drowsy eyes, Isabelle could see that the cabin had a simple, rustic layout. The room where she'd slept with the girls was more of an alcove curtained off from the larger living area. There was also a small kitchenette and a bathroom. Beyond the living room, the outside deck was covered in at least two feet of snow, indicating that no one had used it in a long while. The sun was just rising, casting light through branches that sparkled and shimmered with their icy coating.

Adam stood in the far corner, talking into his phone, Chance at his feet. Isabelle could only make out scraps of the conversation, but it was enough to confirm he was speaking with Nate. A different sort of chill shivered through her. Was there any news?

Adam stared out the window, so deep in conversation that she assumed he hadn't heard her, but she was wrong. As she moved to the counter and poured a mug of coffee from the steaming pot, his voice dropped so she could no longer hear.

What information was he exchanging with Nate that he didn't want her to know? Fear for Jess suddenly warred with concern for their own safety. Isabelle knew she'd had little choice, but she had willingly placed their lives in the hands of a man she knew next to nothing about.

She sipped the coffee and tried to force a semblance of calm to her anxious thoughts. Adam had proved nothing if not that he was selfless and responsible. She had nothing to fear from him...right?

A memory of his panic attack flashed before her eyes, followed quickly by a surge of guilt.

He suffered PTSD, and had apparently lived as a hermit, yet he'd been willing to risk his own mental health for their safety. Thinking of how gentle and funny he'd been with Mia made her want to know more about him. What reservoirs of strength did he carry that allowed him to submerge his own needs in favor of protecting and comforting a frightened child?

She owed him at least a measure of trust.

Isabelle stared out the kitchenette window as she waited for him to finish the call. Fresh snow had fallen overnight, covering their footprints up to the cabin. It was as if they'd never come this way at all. She pulled the blanket closer and cradled the warm coffee mug between her hands as her mind considered how easy it would be to erase their entire existence. As easily as gentle snow erased their footprints.

"Whatever you're thinking, it isn't that bad."

Isabelle started at the sound of Adam's voice close beside her. Thank goodness she had him to protect them, because she was obviously not good at staying alert.

"I'm thinking a blueberry muffin would go great with this coffee." She turned and pasted a smile on her face. "Not that I'm not grateful for the coffee," she amended quickly.

"I can offer a granola bar."

Her smile turned genuine. "Perfect."

He opened a cupboard and pulled out a box. "Your choice. Chocolate chip, chocolate almond or double chocolate chip?"

"Someone likes chocolate."

"It's a universal favorite, so I keep them stocked."

All the questions she had been too tired to think of last night rushed to her mind as she bit into the bar. "What is this place?"

"It's a long story. Short version is, I like to hike and it's good to have a safe place to spend the night if necessary."

Isabelle wanted to know more about that long story, but it was clearly something he wasn't ready to share.

"We need to talk."

The abrupt change and Adam's sudden matter-of-fact tenor unnerved her. Instantly gone was the gentle man who had teased Mia. This was the soldier again, the man she could picture commanding a team. "Is there news?"

"Not yet. Are the children still asleep?"

Isabelle's nerves frayed even more. "They were when I got up. I imagine they'll be out for a while given how late it was when we got here."

"Let's go sit by the window so we don't wake them."

The bite of granola stuck in her throat. She liked friendly Adam much better.

There was a sofa across from the windows and a chair set catty-cornered. Adam stood by the chair and indicated she should sit on the sofa. She sat, pulling her blanket closer and wishing the soft cushions would envelop her.

"Adam, you're scaring me. What's going on?"

He took a sip of his own coffee then set it aside before answering. "We don't know what's going on. That's the problem. Nate has heard nothing. There's been no ransom, no sign of an abandoned car, no witnesses to a struggle. If not for the call you received, it would appear Jess simply vanished into thin air."

Isabelle set her coffee down before her trembling hands could drop the mug. She sank deeper into the cushions and hugged her arms to her chest.

"I need you to tell me everything you know about her."

The gruff tone of his voice startled her. Suddenly, she started to shake as she remembered Nate's questions. "You think she's involved in something bad."

Adam gave her a direct look. "She's definitely involved in something bad. The question is—was it voluntary or not?"

A tear ran down Isabelle's cheek, quickly followed by another. She could not believe this nightmare. As if on cue, Laura began to cry. "I have to get her before she wakes Mia."

Adam stood. "I'll get her while you fix a bottle. Then we'll talk."

Isabelle stumbled into the kitchen area and fumbled with the diaper bag. Tears were streaming in earnest now, and she could barely see what she was doing. Swiping the wetness away with the edge of her sleeve, she took the bottle, measured the scoops of formula, and opened a bottle of water to mix it.

She shook the baby bottle and wiped up the mess she'd made with her unsteady hands. When she turned back, Adam had Laura on the sofa, cooing to her as he changed her diaper. Isabelle's head spun as Adam morphed back into their caregiver.

She brought the bottle to the sofa. Adam handed over Laura without a word, then went to grab the coffee pot. After topping off both of their mugs, he sat down across from her again. Isabelle couldn't bring herself to meet his gaze, but she felt its heat.

When he spoke, his voice was gentler. "Isabelle, I don't have to tell you how serious this situation is."

She nodded. "Yeah, I think I've got that."

"In order to figure out what happened, we need to know more about Jess, about her life, her background. You're the only one who can help with that. I want you to tell me everything you know about her."

Isabelle gazed down at the sweet baby guzzling her bottle, and her heart broke. "I want to help. Truly, I do. But I don't know where to start."

Adam leaned forward, elbows on his knees, and steepled his fingers. "How long have you known her?"

"A year. Maybe less." She paused to do the mental calculation. The two of them had formed a bond so quickly that it shocked her to realize it had been a much shorter time. "About ten months."

That seemed to surprise him.

"It feels like so much longer," she added weakly.

"How did you meet?"

"Mia and I lived in Oklahoma. My husband was stationed there. After he died, I was grief-stricken." She bowed her head, not wanting him to see the wave of emotion she was sure was visible on her face thinking of that awful time.

"You met Jess in Oklahoma?"

"No." Isabelle shook her head and forced herself to focus on the task. "Once Daniel was gone, I had no place there anymore. People were kind, but I felt uncomfortable, like I was a reminder of the worst that could happen." Her voice faltered.

"So, you came here? What made you choose Colorado?"

She smiled sadly, gave a half laugh. "It wasn't so much that I chose Colorado as my car chose for me. It sounds like such a cliché. My car broke down, I fell in love with the town, and I stayed."

She fidgeted with the blanket Laura was wrapped in. Adam waited patiently.

"That would be the simple answer. The deeper one is that I was in a really bad place emotionally. My husband was dead, and I was lost. I didn't know how to move forward beyond the day-to-day care of my daughter. I wasn't functioning as the mother Mia needed. I knew it wasn't fair to her for me to live in the past. She had a future, even if I didn't, and I needed to help her embrace it. So, I decided to make a fresh start. I had no idea where to go, but I decided to consider it an adventure. We'd drive until we found someplace that felt like home." She paused for a moment, looking for the right words to continue.

"Danny would have laughed at me because I was always such a planner—every minute of our lives, our future planned out and tracked on spreadsheets." She shrugged helplessly. "That obviously didn't work, so I decided to place my trust in God and my faithful car." She laughed. "I still trust God."

Adam sucked in a breath at the simple faith of her declaration. She was trying to make him laugh, but instead she'd revealed so much of herself to him. He hated doing this, making her revisit such a traumatic time in her life, but they needed something to go on, some information to help figure out what had happened to Jess and who was after Isabelle and the children. He deliberately ignored the uncomfortable twinge he'd felt hearing her talk about her dead husband, and pushed on. "Then what happened?"

"That's when I met Jess. I had the car towed to a service station and was looking for some place to wait. Jess was helping out in the gardens at the church when I wandered in to pray. Mia started chatting with her, telling her all about our car woes, and, before I knew it, Jess had offered me a room in the parish guesthouse and—"

"Wait, the parish has a guesthouse?" Adam had lived on the outskirts of this town for years, but it was a sign of his reclusive life that he had no idea what she was talking about.

Isabelle smiled and his heart lit up in response. "It's called Samaritan Home—you know, after the parable. It's a place where anyone down on their luck can find welcome for however long they need it. Jess said she'd stayed there when she first got to town, so she could recommend it."

Adam promised himself he'd find out more about Samaritan Home from Nate, but right now he focused on what Isabelle had said about Jess. "So, she was new to town also? When did she arrive?"

Isabelle's face fell. "Sorry, I don't know. I think I didn't realize at first that she hadn't been there long. She seemed so at home in that garden—almost like she'd grown up there. She knew the pastor well. I didn't really think about it at the time. I guess I imagined her coming here as a child. It was only later, when she made a comment in passing, that I realized she had only come to town recently. Ironically, we had very similar situations—though her car hadn't broken down. But that's what Jess is like. She seemed like she'd been here forever because she makes friends easily wherever she goes. People love her."

Her voice cracked, but Adam forced himself to deepen

the probe. He had too many questions to stop because this was upsetting her. Their safety had to be his priority. "What about Laura's father?"

"I don't know. I didn't ask."

Adam was incredulous. "Why not?"

Isabelle got defensive. "Because it isn't my business to ask people to divulge their darkest secrets to strangers they've just met."

He acknowledged that. "But later, when you came to be friends, she didn't say anything then?"

"No." She shrugged. "We were too busy with our current lives to talk about the past. Though…"

"Yes?"

"You asked if I noticed anything."

He waited.

"Sometimes when I'd come upon her sitting with Laura, she would be staring out into the forest as if she was thinking of something that made her very sad." Isabelle cuddled Laura a little closer.

"But you don't know what it was? You didn't ask?"

"I did once, but she denied there was anything wrong, said she had dust in her eyes. I took that as a request not to pry."

Adam's frustration grew. There had to be something here he could use. "Let's go back over yesterday morning. Tell me again what happened."

Isabelle sighed and shifted the baby. "Jess called and said she had a sudden appointment in the morning, and could I possibly come watch Laura. Of course, I said yes. That's what we did for each other. If I'd asked, she'd have done the same. We were two single mothers who had become close friends and we relied on each other for everything."

"She never mentioned family?"

Isabelle bit down on her lip. "Only to say she didn't have

any. It was when we were trying to decide what to do about Christmas. She said she had no family, so she and Laura were on their own. That's when we decided to spend it together."

"When did she ask you to become Laura's guardian?"

Isabelle thought back. "About two weeks ago."

She stood to burp Laura and began pacing the room with the baby on her shoulder. "I wondered what made her ask. She said she felt vulnerable as a single parent. Who would care for Laura if something happened to her? Who could she rely on?"

"Did she indicate she had some reason for worrying?"

"No. I assumed it had something to do with our conversations about family, about feeling vulnerable as single parents. We'd talked a lot about that over Christmas."

Adam stared out the window, pondering what she'd said. It all made sense in a way. He understood that if Jess was keeping life-threatening secrets, she wouldn't have wanted anyone to know. She provided for her daughter's safety, which was her main concern. Except, there was one thing she apparently hadn't considered. She hadn't factored in that whoever was a threat to her, was also a threat to Laura and, by extension, to Isabelle and Mia.

Adam's ringing phone interrupted his thoughts.

"Yes, Nate?"

As he talked, he surreptitiously watched Isabelle. She was upset, which was understandable. He'd asked some deeply personal questions. And yet, despite all his questioning, he had no more answers than he'd begun with. In fact, he only had more questions, the biggest one of all being whether to trust Isabelle's answers. He believed one hundred percent that she sincerely cared for Laura and was terrified of the men chasing them. What he couldn't ascertain was if she was being truthful with her responses about Jess. She was definitely terrified for her friend. But could she also be covering for her?

SIX

"We need to pack up and move out."

Isabelle stopped midstride. She'd been pacing the room with Laura as she'd tried to process all the questions Adam had posed. She was still reeling, not so much from his questions, though, as from the realization they'd forced on her—how little she really knew her friend. She'd thought of them as so close, sharing everything, but Jess had obviously been keeping secrets.

"Isabelle?"

She shook herself. "Sorry. What did you say?"

"That we have to leave. The tires on my SUV are shredded, so Nate is going to meet us out by the road. It will be a hike, though. Maybe half an hour, so we need to get going."

Her body and mind screamed in rebellion at the idea of another hike through the woods. Every muscle ached from all the running yesterday. It didn't matter. Reminding herself that these men were trying to keep her alive, and not wanting to show him any weakness, Isabelle just nodded. "I'll wake Mia."

While Mia ate a granola bar and drank water, Isabelle packed up the few belongings she'd brought. Within twenty minutes, they were ready to go.

Something was different, though. She couldn't put a finger on it precisely, but the tension that had arisen between them this morning lingered in the air. Of course, Adam was still kind with Mia, walking with her perched on his shoulders. Isabelle could hear them whispering, and she could see Adam's arm extend as he pointed to things in the forest. Isabelle smiled. Mia would be eating up the attention. Isabelle was struck again by how different her life and Mia's might have been if Daniel had been open to treatment like Adam clearly was.

As she trudged along behind Adam and Mia, with only the monotony of her own thoughts for company, Isabelle searched her memory. What did she know of Jess's past? It was hard not to wish she'd dug deeper, thought to question, but the truth was she hadn't asked any questions because she hadn't wanted Jess asking them of her in return.

Isabelle buried the troubling thoughts. They weren't relevant. It wasn't her past that Adam was questioning. Her failed marriage was no concern of his, because it had no bearing on his need to keep them safe. She hadn't shared any of those details with Jess either. Which left her wondering... What details about her past had Jess deliberately not shared? Who was Laura's father? Did he have anything to do with the current threat?

Pressure on Isabelle's leg startled her. She glanced down to see Chance nuzzling her thigh. He looked up at her almost as if he sensed her sadness. Was it possible? She bent down to ruffle his golden fur.

As she straightened, Chance ran ahead to Mia and Adam and tugged on Adam's pant leg. Adam turned to look back. Isabelle laughed. "I think he's telling you to wait up for the slowpoke."

Adam slowed and waited for her to catch up. "We're almost to the edge of the road, but I want to stay within the tree line until Nate gets here."

"You think we're still being followed?"

"I don't want to take any chances. There was no one following us in the woods, but…" He shrugged.

It was only then Isabelle realized that, while Adam may have been chatting with Mia, his eagle-eyed attention had been on their surroundings. And Chance had also been working. Together they'd been engaged in constant surveillance. All while she'd been lost in thoughts of the past. It was time to clear her head and focus on staying alive.

"Where is Nate taking us?"

"He said to the station. I think he wants to go over some things with you."

More questions. Isabelle's brain ached.

She heard the sound of an approaching car just as Adam's phone buzzed. She started toward the road, but he put an arm out to hold her back.

"Yes?… Got it."

He closed the phone. "Deeper into the forest—fast." He was guiding her behind the trees even as he gave the command.

"I take it that car is not Nate."

"No. Nate said he realized he was being tailed so he pulled over. The car passed him and headed our way."

"How was he being tailed?"

"Anyone can pick up a tail. Nate's an experienced army ranger and sheriff. If he thinks he was being tailed, A—they're good and B—he's right. But because he's experienced, he knew how to lose them before he got to us."

Adam lowered Mia to the ground and had them duck behind a thick cluster of trees. "Chance, stay. Protect."

"Where are you going?" Isabelle couldn't help the panic that infused her voice.

"I just want to get closer to the road to get details on the car. I won't be visible to them, and I'll be right back."

Isabelle peered through the branches. True to his word,

Adam melted into the forest thanks to the camouflage pattern of his coat. She was grateful for the dark brown coat he'd given her too. If nothing else, she could pass as a tree trunk.

The silly thought prompted a slightly hysterical giggle. She tried to swallow it, but Mia heard. "What's so funny, Mommy?"

Isabelle crouched beside her daughter and whispered into her ear, "We look like part of the trees. Let's hope no birds decide to make a nest in our hair." Mia's reaction simultaneously warmed and broke her heart. Her little girl laughed, but she did it in a whisper.

Isabelle's heart stuttered. *Oh, Jess. What have you gotten us involved with?*

Adam stood within the tree line, waiting. He hadn't wanted to divulge to Isabelle how concerned he was by the persistent tracking. He needed time to talk to Nate alone, get a sense of what his buddy was thinking.

He stilled as the car that Nate had described came into view. If he hadn't been suspicious from Nate's description, the slow speed would have given it away. As beautiful as this forest was to him, there was nothing to make the average driver proceed so slowly unless he was searching for something.

And that something was Isabelle and the girls.

Thinking ahead to assess all possible outcomes was part of his training and, right now, he knew one thing. They needed a better plan. Waiting for Nate and then taking the time to get everyone settled into his car was too risky. Who knew when the driver might decide to circle back? He sent a text to Nate, telling him to wait where he was. He'd get Isabelle and the girls and meet him there.

Adam was headed back through the trees when the first sharp pain sliced through his head. His breath caught as his vision blurred. He slumped against the nearest tree trunk and closed his eyes.

Burying his head in his hands, he tried to massage away the stabbing pain. He was used to headaches. They were an annoying constant reminder of his brain injury. They'd gotten slightly better when Chance had come into his life.

Despite the pain, he smiled thinking of his buddy. Everything was better with Chance around.

The fact that this headache was so strong was an indication of the toll these events were taking on him. Like being back in action, muscle memory had his body responding to the threat with heightened senses. His body was on high alert. He massaged his temples again, but it didn't stop the pounding pain. What he really needed was an ice pack, his bed, and a darkened room. With none of those available to him, Adam knew he had only one option. He usually avoided relying on medication because he didn't want to spend his life hooked on pain pills. But there were times it was unavoidable, and this was one. He needed to be able to concentrate. Surrendering to the need, he dug into his backpack for the pill and swallowed it with a swig of water from a canteen at his hip. He pushed away from the tree and took some deep breaths, waiting for the meds to kick in and the pain to subside.

The sound of an approaching car pulled him out of himself. It was the same car, on its way back. Had the driver seen something? Had Isabelle or the girls moved?

Swiftly but silently, his heart pounding in tune with his head, he darted through the forest, breathing a sigh of relief only when he came to the clearing and found them hidden where he'd left them. Crouching down beside Isabelle, he uttered a prayer of gratitude before whispering directions.

"We have to go back into the forest and work our way around to Nate."

The look on her face told him she understood even as she asked, "He's looking for us?"

Adam nodded. "We can't risk going out to the road. I told Nate where to meet us. It's a parking lot hunters use, but since it's not in season, we're okay."

"How far?"

Adam saw the fatigue in her eyes even though she tried to make the question casual. "About ten minutes, give or take."

Isabelle nodded.

"Why don't we switch off? Mia can walk with you, and I'll take Laura." He didn't want to admit that carrying Mia on his shoulders was a problem, but the medication sometimes threw his balance off and he didn't want to risk falling with her perched up high.

Isabelle nodded. She handed the baby over and took Mia by the hand. They set off through the forest on a path at a diagonal to the road. True to his estimate, it took only ten minutes despite their flagging energy.

Once Nate had Isabelle and the girls settled into the car, he turned to Adam. "You okay?"

"Yeah, just a headache."

Nate looked at him with knowing eyes. "How bad?"

"I'll live."

"Need me to take them into protective custody?"

"Not yet."

Nate stood with his arms folded across his chest but nodded. His friend knew better than to try to talk him out of this. "What's the plan?"

"I was going to take them to the station, go over things, but this tail makes me think we need a change of plans."

A sense of unease churned in Adam's gut. "You think there's a leak?"

"Don't know." Nate shrugged. "Since I don't, it seems best we go somewhere else. What about Claire's?"

Adam was surprised by the suggestion. His sister Claire ran a dog training center just on the other side of town. "I don't know. I don't want to bring danger down on Claire and the dogs."

"Just until I can find a safe house—and figure out what's going on."

"Let me check with Claire."

"Already did. She's waiting for us."

Adam eyed his friend with raised eyebrows.

"What? She's happy to help. Says she knows both Jess and Isabelle from church."

That was something new to ponder. Adam climbed into the sheriff's vehicle, wondering if his sister could possibly shed any light on the situation with Jess.

"Where are we going?"

Adam recognized the blend of fear and tension in Isabelle's voice and reminded himself how difficult it must be for her to have lost total control of any aspect of her life. He understood that feeling all too well. "We're headed to my sister's ranch. I think Mia will enjoy it," he added.

"Isabelle, I have some good news," Nate interjected as they came to a stop at a light. "My deputy found something of yours." He reached to hand her a bag with her phone.

"Oh, thank you. Where was it?"

"In the bushes under the window."

"That makes sense. I guess it slipped from my pocket when I was climbing out the window. Please tell him thank you for me."

"Will do. When we get to Claire's, I'd like to see the texts Jess sent you."

"Okay. There's a new one here now."

"What?" Nate whipped his head around. "What does it say?"

"The tree holds all the answers."

Adam frowned. "What does that mean?"

Isabelle shrugged. "I have no clue, but it means she's alive, right?"

Nate swung the car down a long driveway. The sound of barking dogs was the first indication they'd arrived. Adam smiled despite his residual headache when he saw Mia's eyes light up.

"My sister runs a dog rescue. This is where Chance came from." He was gratified to see the tension ease from Isabelle's face as she watched her daughter's excitement. As dangerous as the circumstances were, Isabelle had to also be concerned about the long-term effects all this may have on her daughter. Claire and her dogs would be a welcome distraction. But as they got out of the car, and Chance bounded alongside Mia to meet Claire, he reminded himself that he couldn't afford to be distracted. The girls' lives depended on him.

Claire came out to greet them and, after being nearly toppled by an enthusiastic Chance, she warmly welcomed Isabelle and Mia. She then turned and threw herself into his arms. Her hug was fierce, and when she drew back, Adam saw the sheen in her eyes.

"It's good to have you here."

Embarrassed, knowing her heart was in the right place, but that her assessment of the situation was overly optimistic, Adam quickly shifted the tone. "Thank you for being willing to take us in."

Claire was, by nature, alert to nuances in body language and expression. Adam knew it was one of the qualities that made her so good with dogs. In this case, it let her quickly pick up on his subtext. She turned her attention back to her guests.

"Why don't you come in and let me get you settled? I've

got soup warming because you must be cold and starved." She spoke to Mia, "I hope you like grilled cheese."

Lunch was followed by a tour of the facilities while Claire explained how she took in rescue dogs and trained them for a variety of tasks. Some became therapy animals like Chance, but others went on for additional training to work with police or fire canine units.

Adam appreciated all his sister was doing to help her guests feel at home, but he needed time and access to a computer. When Isabelle suggested she put the girls down for a nap, Adam seized the opportunity to go work in Claire's office. He wanted to see what he could find out about Jess's background.

Half an hour later, frustration growing, he sat back in the chair and ran his hands through his already tousled hair. Feeling eyes on him, he turned to see Isabelle standing in the doorway with mugs of steaming coffee. "Claire needed to attend to the dogs, but she thought you might appreciate some fuel for your brain."

His sister also seemed to think she was a matchmaker. As Adam accepted the coffee, he made a mental note to set Claire straight. "Thanks. Maybe it will clear my head."

"How's your headache?"

He stopped with the mug at his lips and stared at her over the rim. "What did Claire say?"

"Nothing. I recognized the signs. Daniel used to get headaches too."

Something in the way her face held stiff as she responded prompted him to ask, "How did he cope with them?"

She dropped her gaze and he could no longer see the expression in her eyes. She shrugged. "Different ways. Sometimes he—"

Almost simultaneously, a cacophony of barking erupted

from the kennels and a heart-stopping scream emanated from down the hall.

Isabelle dropped the mug of coffee, oblivious to the splatter of hot liquid and the shattering cup as she whirled and raced through the doorway, Adam right on her heels. Chance bounded past them both and tore into the room where Isabelle had left the girls to rest.

"He took Laura!"

Mia's words reached him, pushing Adam to run faster. By the time he made the doorway, Chance had a grip on the pant leg of a man climbing through the window, Laura in his arms. Adam dashed across the room, yanked the man back by his coat, and snatched Laura from his arms. He handed the baby over to Isabelle while Chance kept his grip on the man's pant leg. "Take the girls and go call Nate. Chance and I have him."

"Think again," the man growled. With a quick jerk, he grabbed the standing lamp and swung it at Chance. Instinctively, Adam threw himself between his dog and the attacker, taking the brunt of the impact. The man took advantage, yanking his pants free and catapulting through the open window in one smooth move.

Adam glanced at Isabelle standing frozen in the doorway. "In the kitchen, there's a phone with a direct line to the kennels. Call Claire. Tell her to let the dogs loose. Then call Nate." Without waiting for a response, he launched himself through the window with Chance following on his heels.

SEVEN

Adam landed in the snow. He rolled and bounced back up to his feet and took off after the would-be abductor. The man had a head start, and was properly outfitted for the weather, but Adam was not about to let the lack of a coat or shoes hinder him from pursuing this man who had attempted to kidnap an innocent baby. Capturing him would give them their first real break in this case.

That thought gave Adam an extra spurt of energy, but without shoes, his socked feet kept slipping in the snow. He was losing ground. Then the sound of an engine caught his ear. There was a road running behind the ranch, so the engine raised a concern. Did this guy have an accomplice waiting for him? Knowing he needed to run faster, Adam paused long enough to pull off his thick socks before launching himself forward again. He had to catch the man before he reached the road.

Adam gained ground as the man made for the tree line. He abruptly turned to the right seconds before gunshots from the woods peppered the ground around Adam. With an accomplice confirmed, Adam began zigzagging to avoid the gunman's aim, but he was losing precious ground in the process.

His hopes were sinking fast. There was no way he could reach the man in time. But with his adversary mere steps from the road and freedom, Adam felt a sudden change in the air and realized Claire had unleashed the pack of dogs. A wild flurry of animals flew across the lawn. Adam recognized three that she was training for K-9 suspect apprehension. As Claire called commands, they raced past Adam, surrounding the man and forcing him away from the road. They formed a circle around him, snarling and holding him captive as surely as any handcuffs could have done.

The sound of the car receded and Adam chuckled. It seemed there was no honor among kidnappers. This man had been left to take the fall all on his own.

Claire strolled up beside him, holding out a pair of boots and a leash. Once Adam's feet were protected, she commanded the dogs to sit and signaled to Adam that he could enter the circle.

He smiled as he accepted the leash to secure the prisoner. "Nice work, sis."

Adam turned to the man, who stood in stony silence, still warily eyeing the dogs. "Who are you? What do you want with Isabelle and the children?"

The man glared back at him but maintained his silence.

"Have it your way." He turned back to Claire. "Maybe the dogs would like to encourage him to walk around the front of the house?"

At Claire's command, the dogs fell in around them. With the canine escorts nudging, they forced the man back across the lawn to the house, arriving just as Nate's vehicle pulled up.

Nate stepped out and stood, hands on hips, chuckling. "Isabelle said you needed help, but I guess she was wrong."

"Claire and her dogs get full credit. You should have her train one for you." Adam noticed a blush sneak up his sister's face as Nate hung his head and shuffled his feet. Adam was struck by the suspicion he'd missed something. Was there more than friendship between his sister and his friend? His speculations were interrupted when another official-looking car pulled up behind the sheriff's.

Nate took custody of the alleged kidnapper and read him his rights while Adam focused on the woman who emerged from the car.

"Who is she?"

Nate stared straight ahead as he held the rear car door open for the now-handcuffed captive. His voice was barely audible. "She's the intake caseworker for child welfare."

Adam's heart sank. "She's not here to take Laura, is she? Did you call her? Why'd you do that? Isabelle will be crushed."

Nate shrugged, but Adam heard the strain in his voice as he replied. "She was with me when the call came in. Asked about the case and then insisted she had to come see to the safety of the baby."

Adam stared after the somber woman who was now following Claire up the path. He forced his emotions under control. "You can't let her take Laura, Nate. This attempted abduction changes everything." The thought crystalized even as he said the words. "They're not after Isabelle. They want Laura. I'm sure of it." He paused. "I just don't know why."

"I might have the answer to that, but let me take this guy in first and see what I can get out of him. I'll be back later."

Adam didn't like to be left hanging, especially with the caseworker here, but he could follow up with Nate later. It was more important that he get inside and support Isabelle right now. He had to make the caseworker see reason. He couldn't let her take Laura into her care because, if he was right, that would be a deadly mistake.

This attempted abduction had just proved that Laura was the one who needed his protection most.

* * *

Isabelle paced the room with Laura on her shoulder as she spoke with the woman. What was her name? Isabelle searched her memory but couldn't remember. Her brain had ceased to function the minute the woman had introduced herself as the caseworker here to take custody of Jess's daughter. Alice? Yes, that was it. She'd said her name was Alice Grant, but to Isabelle she was just another person who was a threat to Laura. Isabelle walked to the window and shifted Laura to the other shoulder, trying to buy some time. Where were Adam and Nate? She needed their support.

"Ms. Weaver, without proof that you have legal custody, I am required to remove the child…for her own safety."

Shivers raced through Isabelle's body and she hugged Laura closer, as if by the sheer force of her love she could change the outcome. "I showed you the text from Jess."

"I'm sorry. That's not enough, given the circumstances."

"I told you. There are guardianship papers. Jess appointed me to be Laura's guardian."

"I need to see the papers."

Panicked, Isabelle tried to remember what Jess had said. With her lawyer, right? She glanced at her phone to check the time and her heart sank as she noticed the date. Sunday. It was highly unlikely she could reach the lawyer on a Sunday.

She knew this woman was trying to do the right thing, but taking Laura from the only family she had left was not it. Frantic, she tried to think. "I can call the lawyer in the morning. He'll have the papers…" Her voice trailed off as the caseworker shook her head.

"Please understand, Ms. Weaver. I am not trying to be difficult. It is my responsibility to see to the child's safety."

"I love her like my own daughter. I will keep her safe." Isabelle was desperate now. "She knows me. She feels safe with me. Her mother is my very best friend. I would do anything to keep her from harm."

"But you can't promise that, can you? Someone who is after you just tried to abduct her. If you truly love her, you will agree that me taking her is the only correct choice."

Terror seized Isabelle at the caseworker's words and her thoughts flew to Mia. Praise the Lord, Claire had left with a whispered promise to take Mia to the kennels. Did Alice know about Mia? Because, based on her comments, the next logical step would mean the caseworker would be taking her daughter, as well, for her safety of course. She couldn't let that happen. She couldn't lose Mia or Laura.

But then Alice's words echoed again in her heart. *If you truly love her…* A tear slid down her cheek, plopping on Laura's head. The baby looked up, started. As Isabelle stared into her precious face, so much like a mini-Jess, confusion overcame her. She wanted what was best for this child, but how could she possibly know what that was?

"Why do you think she will be safer with you?"

"Ms. Weaver, I was with the sheriff when he got your call. This child's life was just in danger because of the men after you! You can't properly protect her."

"You're wrong."

Adam's voice rang out so strong and clear that Isabelle latched onto it with actual physical relief. She cuddled Laura to her chest as Adam strode across the room toward the caseworker.

"Former army ranger Adam Dalton." He extended his hand and waited. Isabelle bit back a smile. Her own personal knight in shining army fatigues to the rescue. Not that he was actually in uniform, but despite his jeans and heavy sweater, he carried himself in a way that bespoke his former rank. The presence of her gallant rescuer sent a flood of relief through Isabelle's body.

Alice accepted his handshake but challenged his words. "How can you say I'm wrong? This baby was almost kidnapped."

Isabelle hugged Laura even closer as she protested. "But Adam rescued her. He risked his own life to save her."

She could tell from Alice's raised brows that her argument was futile.

Adam moved to stand beside Isabelle and rested a hand on her arm to steady her. He took a moment to look deeply into her eyes, and her body began to calm.

He stroked Laura's head; his touch so gentle, Isabelle felt it like a balm to her soul.

He turned back to the caseworker. "You're wrong about Isabelle being the target. The real target is this baby."

Isabelle gasped. Her legs went weak and she sank into a chair as calm deserted her.

Adam cleared his throat and continued. "Nate took the prisoner in for interrogation, but he will confirm this truth. If you take this baby, you are not only putting her life in jeopardy, but you will be putting an innocent foster family in the path of ruthless criminals."

Isabelle started to shake. What was Adam talking about?

"Nate and I will arrange a safe house for Isabelle…and the baby." Adam paused to allow his words to sink in. "I know you'll need more details, but we cannot release them at this point. I'm asking you to trust our judgment as professionals who are used to assessing risks."

Alice was obviously as shocked by Adam's words as she was, but as Isabelle watched, she could see that the caseworker seemed to at least be considering them. For the first time, Isabelle felt like maybe she could breathe again.

"I'll need to confirm with Sheriff Brant." Alice looked at Isabelle. "And I'll need to see those papers."

Isabelle nodded. "I'll contact the lawyer."

Alice stepped into the side room to make her call. When she returned, she cast them an odd look and spoke briskly. "Nate confirmed your concerns." She faced Isabelle. "Based on the sheriff's information, I will leave her with you temporarily, but I will need a copy of the papers the attorney will file with the court to make it permanent. You'll need a criminal background check and..."

Her voice droned on, but Isabelle's brain drowned out the words. She couldn't think about permanent now. Permanent meant not finding Jess. Permanent meant her friend was dead. She wasn't ready to accept permanent yet.

Adam nudged her side and Isabelle jolted. Alice was still speaking.

"These are highly unusual circumstances. Our goal is always to see to the child's best interests. Nate has convinced me you and Adam are the best we can do for Laura. For tonight." She gave a pointed stare. "If anything changes, you will notify me immediately."

Isabelle nodded her assent. Alice seemed to soften. She reached out and stroked a hand over Laura's tiny fist.

"I can tell you truly love her." She smiled sadly. "I hope Nate can find her mother."

Isabelle sniffled and the tears slipped down her cheeks. Something they could agree on.

After Alice left, Isabelle collapsed onto the sofa.

"Adam, what were you talking about? What do you mean Laura is the target?"

"Think about it. That man in custody, he didn't come after you or Mia. He tried to snatch Laura. He was halfway out the window with her when Chance latched onto him."

Isabelle held Laura closer, as if that could somehow remove the threat, but she mulled over Adam's words. "I hate it, but that makes sense. If they were after Jess, then Laura would be next." She looked up at him, knowing it was wrong to drag him deeper into her problems but not knowing where else to turn. "What are we going to do? How can we keep her safe?"

"Let's take it one step at a time. For tonight, Nate is going to send a deputy out to watch the house. Between that, Claire's dogs, Chance, and all of us on alert, she will be safe. In the morning, we'll see what the lawyer says. Maybe he knows Jess's true story."

"Okay." She was talking more to herself. Trying to absorb it all. "Okay. We can do that."

But suddenly everything collapsed in on her and she began trembling.

Adam sat beside her on the sofa and, wrapping his arm around her shoulders, drew her into the shelter of his embrace. The warmth. The safety. His strength. Her emotions were on overdrive. Tears brimmed in her eyes, spilling over and running down her face. She choked back the sobs that threatened to break loose. Adam held her close and soothed her, all the time talking to her in soft words, telling her how lucky Laura was to have her, how brave she was. What a wonderful mother she was to both girls.

Isabelle's head jerked up at that. "Where's Mia?"

Adam smiled and opened his phone to show her a picture of Mia surrounded by puppies. "While Alice was talking to Nate, I texted Claire and asked her to keep Mia down there."

"Thank you." The sobs built in her throat again. "I was so scared Alice was going to take Laura, and then when she started talking about the danger, I was afraid she would take Mia too." Isabelle took a deep breath and forced herself to relax, tried to smile. "And then you came in and saved the day."

Adam laughed softly and the sound eased her tension.

"I didn't even thank you for before, for rescuing her." She looked up at Adam, knowing admiration was shining in her eyes, but not even trying to hide it. "I don't even have words to make you understand what it means to me. You've been amazing with everything you've done for us, but the way you dove through that window and took off after the kidnapper..." She paused and blinked, still in awe of his quick action. "You risked your life for Laura, for a little girl you've known less than forty-eight hours."

Their faces were so close as Adam bent over Laura and tickled her little toes that Isabelle could feel his indrawn breath, the sudden burst of tension, and just as quickly, she felt his exhale. Isabelle looked up as Adam looked down, and a long moment passed between them. He winked at her. "Anything for my football baby."

EIGHT

The sound of sleet hitting the windows woke Isabelle, but she refused to open her eyes. It would take a month of uninterrupted sleep to recover from the past two days. And it wasn't over yet. This morning she had a meeting scheduled with Jess's lawyer. Once she'd found the email last night, she'd contacted the lawyer. The fact that he had responded so quickly on a Sunday evening had both alarmed and relieved her. Maybe he knew something. Maybe she could at last get some answers, something to help them understand what this was all about.

The horror of the previous night came washing over her. She had come so close to losing Laura. And Mia! Her daughter had been so brave but, as a mother, it was terrifying to think of her child challenging a kidnapper. Isabelle rolled over, ready to snuggle with her precious girl before facing what promised to be another long and dangerous day.

Her arm met empty air as she rolled to her side. Where was Mia? Panic surged and she bolted upright, her gaze searching room.

Laura was still asleep in the crib. That meant everything was okay, right? Adam had decided Laura was the target, not Isabelle, not Mia. So, if Laura was still safe…

Isabelle's panicked thoughts raced ahead as she pulled on a

heavy robe and started for the door. She caught herself. No, she couldn't leave Laura alone. She gently lifted the infant, cradling her as she hurried into the hall, calling for her daughter.

The sound of Adam's voice drew her toward the kitchen. She burst through the doorway with Laura, her gaze raking the room. "Where's Mia?"

Adam intercepted her before she got far. "She's fine, Isabelle. She's having breakfast and coloring."

Isabelle peered around him, needing to see for herself. Sure enough, Mia was sitting at the table with a stack of drawings beside her.

She exhaled slowly and suddenly her legs couldn't hold her. Adam caught her by the elbow and steadied her. "She's fine," he repeated softly. "She woke up early and was hungry."

Isabelle tried to focus on breathing before approaching Mia. The last thing she wanted to do was to frighten her daughter. When she felt steady, she looked up at Adam, intending to thank him, but the intensity of his gaze made her wobble again. She sucked in a breath, nodded, and pulled away to go to her daughter.

"Good morning, sweetie." She leaned over to kiss the top of Mia's head, and the sweet scent of rose shampoo filled her head, centering her. "What are you drawing?"

Mia squirmed around in her chair and grinned up at her. "Hi, Mama. Mr. Adam remembered to bring my crayons. He said I should draw what scared me. See?"

Isabelle glanced at the pictures—a child's view of the man climbing out the window with a baby and the dog tugging on his pants. There were talk bubbles and bright colors and a hero in a cape.

"It's not so scary now," Mia told her solemnly.

Isabelle glanced up, but Adam was busy at the stove. She shook her head, thanking God again for bringing this generous man into their lives. "Mr. Adam had a very good idea. What else did you draw?"

Mia held up a pile of papers. Most had a little girl and a dog. "You like drawing Chance, don't you?"

Mia beamed with pride. "He's Mr. Adam's special dog. I love him."

Isabelle's heart melted.

Adam pushed away from the stove. "Who's ready for pancakes?"

Mia's hand shot up. "I am!"

"Remember, we can't share these with Chance."

Mia nodded. "Chocolate is bad for dogs."

Isabelle stopped flipping through the drawings and looked at Adam, who was advancing with a plate stacked high with pancakes—chocolate-chip pancakes.

The color drained from her face and she suddenly felt lightheaded.

"Isabelle, are you okay?"

The look of concern on Mia's face matched Adam's voice.

Isabelle pulled herself together and forced a smile to her face. "Yes, I just have to go change Laura's diaper." She turned and fled down the hallway.

Back in the relative safety of her room, Isabelle laid Laura back in the crib. With shaking hands, she reached for a clean diaper, but her fingers were trembling too badly to get the package open. Laura was going to start wailing any minute, and she didn't want Adam or Mia coming to investigate. She ran into the bathroom, thrust her hands under cold water, and then splashed more on her face until she felt her heart-rate begin to slow. She leaned on the vanity and stared at her reflection as she forced herself to take deep steady breaths.

When the force of the blood rushing in her ears eased, she could hear the murmur of voices from down the hall,

Mia's high-pitched giggle in response to the low rumble of Adam's voice.

She closed her eyes, took a breath. In for three, hold for four, out for five. Repeat. And repeat. Slowly, her body eased.

Mia was safe. She was with Adam, a man risking his life to save her. A man who made her pancakes. A man who faced his post-traumatic stress rather than drinking his way through it. Adam was not Daniel. Mia was not in danger—from him.

She turned into the bedroom and on steadier legs walked back to Laura. She leaned over the makeshift crib and tickled her tummy until Laura gurgled happy sounds. Once she had the clean diaper in place, she lifted the infant and cuddled her to her chest. "Sweet baby, I'm going to make sure you are safe until we find your mama. No one is going to take you away from me." She started humming a tune that had always soothed Mia. "Hush little baby," she crooned as she gently rocked the baby.

A sound in the hall caught her attention and she looked up to find Adam standing in the doorway with a mug of coffee and a plate of toast. "I thought you might need something before we left for the lawyer's office. Laura's bottle is warming."

What had she ever done to deserve this wonderful man? She sighed softly as she raised her eyes to his face. "Thank you."

He smiled. A gentle smile that reached her soul. "You're very welcome."

"Claire was kind enough to offer me some clean clothes, so I'll dress while the bottle is warming. We should be able to leave soon. Where's Mia?"

A chagrined expression covered his face. "She's with Claire, getting cleaned up. I might have made a mistake with the pancakes. There was syrup everywhere."

Isabelle laughed. "She loves her pancakes and syrup."

He hesitated. "Then I didn't do something wrong feeding her?"

A part of Isabelle wanted to tell him, to trust him, to spill the whole sordid story…but this wasn't the time.

"You did the absolute perfect thing."

He studied her but obviously saw something that decided him against asking anything more. "Enjoy the coffee."

Isabelle sank onto the bed and, as she sipped from the mug, she tried with all her might to forget the last time she'd seen Daniel. The morning Mia had last had chocolate-chip pancakes with her father—right before his reckless drinking almost killed her.

The drive into Breckenridge was tense, sleet making travel hazardous, but it was the prospect of the upcoming meeting that most had their nerves on edge. Even the children were restless in their car seats. Mia would almost certainly have preferred to stay with Claire and the dogs, but after the kidnapping attempt yesterday, Isabelle was not letting either girl out of her sight, and Adam couldn't blame her.

He glanced at her in the seat beside him. Her fingers were tightly clasped in her lap, and he wondered again what had triggered her reaction this morning. Her anxiety at waking up and not finding Mia was understandable, but she'd calmed down and been fine until he'd served breakfast. What had set her off? He'd thought for a moment that she was going to explain when he'd brought her coffee, but she'd clammed up and focused on this trip instead. Adam knew he was the last person to talk about not sharing your deepest thoughts, your fears, but if Isabelle was keeping secrets that could impact this case, he needed to know.

The sun was breaking through the clouds as Adam parked in the lot behind the office building. They walked around to the front so Mia could shake her sillies out. Adam watched Isabelle dancing and singing with the girls on the wet grass, and his heart gave a funny lurch that was followed by a burst of determination. Isabelle was such a generous and loving person, taking in Laura without a second thought, even knowing the risk. He renewed his vow to do whatever it took to return her life to normal. She deserved nothing less than his best, regardless of any personal cost.

The security guard in the lobby waved them through with barely a glance. Lax security set Adam on edge, and he went on full alert as they entered the elevator. Isabelle glanced at him, and he saw that she'd made the same observation.

The elevator chimed their arrival. The doors opened and he took note of the elegant office space as they stepped out into the empty reception area. The elevator doors shut behind them and silence closed in. An eerie silence that had his instincts telegraphing warnings. Shouldn't a law firm, even a small one, be bustling at this time of the morning? Granted the lawyer had given Isabelle a rushed appointment, before office hours, but shouldn't someone have been there to greet them?

"Wait here," Adam whispered so only Isabelle could hear. "Something feels off." His gaze raked the reception area. "Better yet, take them into that ladies' room. Stay there until I come get you."

Isabelle nodded her assent. "Mia, sweetie, come with me while Adam checks us in, okay?" She winked. "I want to change Laura's diaper before we meet the lawyer. Wouldn't want to stink up his fancy office." Mia giggled and followed her mother.

"Wait." He held a finger to his lips and opened the door to the ladies' room. "Anyone in here?" he asked softly. When there was no reply, he stepped inside and quickly scanned the room. He came back out and nodded to Isabelle. Then he winked at Mia. "No one to be offended by stinky diapers."

Once Isabelle and the girls were hidden away, Adam eased himself through the open glass doors that led from reception to the inner offices. There was no sound from within. No tapping fingers on keyboards, no sounds of a printer and, most telling of all, no voices.

Every army ranger instinct was on alert. Yes, it was early, but the open door meant there should be some sign of life. A whiff of freshly brewed coffee scented the air as Adam warily headed down the hallway. But before he could exhale in relief, a different smell, one he recognized from far too many battlefields, stole his breath. He was torn between the need to investigate and an urgency to get Isabelle and the girls away.

Reassuring himself that they were safe in the bathroom, Adam crept forward. A shaft of light shone from the office at the end of the hall, so he headed that way, peeking into every open door he passed. There was no sign of life anywhere, but no sign of any disturbance either.

The coppery tang grew stronger as he neared the end of the hall.

Adam flattened himself against the wall and held still, listening intently for any sound to indicate trouble. He drove all fear for Isabelle from his mind and focused on sensing any other physical presence.

When he felt nothing, he pulled his gun and swung into the doorway.

"Drop your weapons—"

The sight that met his eyes severed his words. A man, presumably the lawyer they were to meet, lay on the floor, blood pooling around his inert body. Again, the urgent need to get Isabelle away overwhelmed Adam. But this man held clues. If there was a chance he was still alive...

Careful not to disturb any evidence, Adam gingerly stepped toward the man. A door slammed in the distance and he froze.

His instinct was to give chase, but those still here needed him more. He knelt and checked for a pulse but felt nothing. He called 9-1-1 to summon help, said a quick prayer for the man, and sent a quick text telling Isabelle to stay.

His years of army training and battlefield experience kicked in as he searched for the source of the blood loss. Based on where the blood continued to pool, he gently lifted the lawyer, for he no longer had any doubt that's who this man was. A gaping hole under his left shoulder blade gave the answer. On the off chance the man was still alive, Adam ripped off his own jacket and sweater. Bunching the sweater as firmly as he could, he wrapped the arms of his jacket around the man, pulling them tight to try to hold the sweater in place. And then he prayed again as he went to wait for the police.

Police and medical technicians soon swarmed the building, and Adam had to stay to answer questions. Relief filled him when he got a text from Isabelle telling him the security guard was going to bring her to a café in the lobby to keep Mia from viewing the crime scene.

He didn't like the idea of being separated from them, but he understood Isabelle's need to protect her daughter from seeing the violence. Mia had already been exposed to far too much for a child of her age.

The elevator door closed behind them. Mia glanced at the security guard and then looked up at Isabelle.

"Mama, where's Adam? Why isn't he with us?"

"He had to stay with the police. They need his help with something."

Mia tugged at her sleeve until Isabelle met her gaze again. "Did something bad happen?"

Isabelle sighed heavily. She set the baby carrier down and wrapped both arms around Mia. "I'm afraid so, baby." She squeezed tight. "But Adam will take care of it. He'll take care of us."

Isabelle could feel the tremors in Mia's body. Her daughter was going to need so much help to get over these experiences once they were safe. And they would be safe. She surprised herself to realize how very much she believed that. She hadn't known Adam more than a few days, but her faith in him hadn't wavered.

Faith. That brought her up short. She should be praying, not relying on Adam, not placing her faith in a man. She was ashamed to realize she hadn't yet said a prayer for the lawyer who'd been injured, maybe dead, nor had she thought to pray to God for guidance.

I'm sorry, Lord. You above all know Your plan for us. Please help me to know what to do. Please help me to know how to deal with Adam.

The elevator dinged their arrival, and she mentally whispered one last prayer as they stepped from the elevator into the building's empty lobby. *Please protect the girls.*

Police had sealed off the building entry, and Isabelle could see a crowd gathered on the sidewalk outside. She turned to the security guard. "I am not taking these children out into that crowd. Is there somewhere else we can go?"

The security guard stopped to check with the police officer standing watch. "There's a small indoor café and atrium on the ground level. It's been sealed off from outside, but the officer said we can wait there," she reported.

Isabelle nodded her agreement. Hopefully, the café was open. She could use some coffee and maybe a muffin would distract Mia, although the idea that a muffin could distract from what had occurred upstairs was absurd.

The café was quiet but open for service, so Isabelle got food and drinks and then settled them at a table in the far corner.

She sipped her coffee and watched Mia feed bits of blueberry muffin to a giggling Laura, while the security guard went over by the windows to make some calls. Isabelle's thoughts kept drifting to what was going on upstairs and the inescapable conclusion that she had brought this on the lawyer with her phone call. Guilt weighed heavily.

"Mama, can we take Laura to look at the flowers?"

Isabelle refocused on Mia. "Hmm?"

Mia pointed at the small fountain in the middle of the room. It was surrounded by pots of poinsettias obviously left over from a Christmas display.

Isabelle didn't like the idea of being out in the open. She'd prefer to stay huddled in their corner. But how much longer would Adam be upstairs?

"It's okay if you don't want to, Mama."

Isabelle wanted to cry at the nervous resignation in her daughter's voice. She couldn't pretend to Mia that everything was okay and then tell her she couldn't even look at flowers around a fountain. Isabelle scanned the nearly empty café. Aside from the workers, who must have been there before the police descended, there was only a line in the courtyard outside as people slowly snaked to the pickup window for their morning coffee. Nothing appeared threatening.

"Do you want to see the pretty flowers, sweetie?" Isabelle cooed as she unstrapped Laura from the baby carrier and shifted her to her hip.

Laura gurgled happily, which made Mia laugh. Isabelle's heart lifted at the joyous sound, and she uttered a prayer of thanksgiving for the resiliency of children.

They walked over to the cascading fountain and Isabelle let the tranquil setting filter through her. The cheerful splash of the water eased her tension, and Mia's sweet voice combining with Laura's bubbly sounds made her smile. Mia had a way of communicating with Laura that she and Jess had never understood.

She snapped a quick photo of the happy girls, hoping to one day be able to share it with Jess. Knowing Adam was probably stressed about being apart from them, she shared the photo with him and sent an accompanying message to reassure him they were safe.

To reassure herself, she searched out the security guard. The woman had moved to the coffee counter and, as Isabelle watched, she grabbed two paper cups and headed for the courtyard exit. She opened the door just enough to hand the cup through to a man standing outside.

After closing the door, the guard turned and walked back to their table. As she sat down, Isabelle realized she'd left all their belongings unattended while she'd let Mia play. Foolish, foolish, she reprimanded herself. But, really, the only things of value were the two precious girls, and they were right with her.

"Mia, I think we need to take Laura back for a bottle."

As they made their way across to the alcove, Isabelle noticed the guard had pulled her chair slightly away from the table, as if she didn't want to crowd them. It was a kind gesture, or maybe she just hadn't planned on doing duty for a woman and kids and wanted some privacy.

Isabelle took a long sip of her coffee as she dug in her bag for Laura's bottle. She pulled out the trusty pad and box of crayons and handed them to Mia. "Why don't you draw the fountain and the pretty flowers?"

Mia's face lit up. "I can add it to my collection."

"What collection?" Isabelle asked absently as she reached for her coffee again. She hoped Adam wouldn't be much longer because she was suddenly so tired.

"The one I'm making for Aunt Jess so I can show her what we did while she was gone."

Isabelle's heart stuttered and her eyes brightened in hope. She needed some of her daughter's optimism right now. She had to believe that Jess was alive and would be back.

She opened her phone to check if Adam had replied, but there was nothing. She sipped the coffee again as Laura drained her bottle, but tremors in her hands sent a frisson of concern down her arm. She set the bottle down and tried to shift Laura to her shoulder to burp her, but her arms suddenly felt too heavy to lift the baby. Her brain was getting foggy. Something was seriously wrong.

She turned to ask the security guard for help, but something in the way the woman was sitting, surreptitiously observing her, jangled warning bells in Isabelle's cloudy brain. She reached for the coffee again, but her hand stilled. Had someone put something in her coffee? She'd felt fine until they'd come back here and sipped it.

There was something shifting at the edge of her thoughts. A memory she couldn't quite grasp. A sense of something important.

Adam. She needed to send a message to Adam.

She reached for her phone, but it fell off the table into her lap. She called to the security guard for help, but the woman just sat there, a smug look on her face. Panic seized Isabelle. With supreme effort, she forced her finger to steady so she could hit the microphone text icon. "I need help. Been drugged. Security guard won't help—"

The phone clattered to the tile floor as a hand wrenched her arm. Her last image as consciousness faded was of the security guard reaching for Laura.

NINE

Adam paced the foyer, waiting for a police update. His phone dinged and he glanced down. A photo of the two girls made him smile, but a second text came through just as he was about to respond.

I need help. Been drugged. Security guard won't—

The nagging unease that had been roiling in his gut burst into full-fledged terror. Adam immediately tried to call, but Isabelle's phone rang through to voice mail. He scanned the room, looking for the security guard who had let them in. He was being questioned by police, so Adam dashed across the room and interrupted.

"The other guard—the one who took the woman and children down to the café—who is she?"

The guard glanced at the officer then shrugged. "Never saw her before. She showed up this morning. Said the regular guard had called out and the agency sent her as a replacement."

Adam's heart started to race. Light danced around the periphery of his eyes and his chest began to tighten. He recognized the signs of an impending attack but fought the rising panic. Isabelle needed him—functioning and able to rescue her. Chance was with Claire, so he had to fight this on his own. He had to. Three lives were at risk.

Just that thought made his chest constrict more and his breathing became labored. He closed his eyes and leaned forward. Resting his hands on his knees, he tried to imagine Chance beside him, bumping his leg, interrupting the panic cycle. He pushed back at the paralyzing thoughts, trying to use the techniques he'd learned. He couldn't surrender to a panic attack when Isabelle's life depended on him. He took a deep breath and forced out the question. "Where's the café?"

"Ground floor. Back side."

"What's this all about?" the cop asked.

Adam turned to the officer and showed him the message. "Call for backup. Is there anyone downstairs? Radio them to get into the café. I think the people who killed the lawyer are trying to kidnap this woman and her children."

The officer got right on the radio but Adam couldn't wait. He pressed the elevator button, but nothing happened.

The security guard called to him. "Take the freight elevator. Back there." He pointed down the hall. "It will exit just behind the café."

Adam ran around to the freight entrance. He hit the call button and watched the display as the elevator ascended, ticking the numbers off in his head at the excruciatingly slow progress, knowing that each passing moment gave the kidnapper time to get away with Laura. A guttural cry locked in his throat at the thought of losing the little girl. Why had he let them out of his sight?

Please, God, let me get to them in time.

The elevator finally reached him. He didn't even wait for the doors to fully open before he slipped through the gap and punched the buttons to close the door and take him down. Like a caged beast, he paced the confines of the small moving room, wanting to pound on something, to do anything to take back his decisions of the last hour that had put Isabelle in danger.

No! Adam brought himself up short. He had to stop this. Rage was no more help than his panic had been. Isabelle and the children needed him to think like the trained warrior he was.

He knew how to do this. He knew how to prepare for a mission. Forcing himself to blank his mind, he exhaled slowly, forcibly expelling the oxygen from his lungs as he focused on tactical breathing until his emotions were locked away and his thoughts were strategic.

When the heavy elevator finally clanged to a halt, Adam was ready. He flattened his body against the side wall and waited for the door to open. He eased forward so he could see around the opening. Continuing to breathe slowly, he focused his attention on the noises coming from the café. As he listened intently, trying to isolate the sounds, he heard a voice he recognized. Mia's cries pierced his heart. His every instinct screamed at him to run to her.

Instead, he forced the pain aside and stealthily made his way down the corridor. He peered through the café door and saw chaos. Discarding his careful plans, he charged through the door. Isabelle was on the ground, surrounded by cops, and Mia was bawling about the baby. He wanted to rush to comfort her, but he saw her pointing to a door at the back of the room. Without a moment's hesitation, Adam pivoted and bolted across the floor toward what looked to be the café kitchen.

He pushed through the door and, with a glance, took in the stunned staff members. "A woman came through here with a baby. Which way did she go?"

A worker pointed a trembling finger to the hallway, but there was no one in sight.

Darkness started to crowd Adam's brain as he scanned the empty hallway. He pushed back, impatient with himself. Which way could she have gone?

"She went the wrong way, into the storeroom."

Adam acknowledged the whispered comment with a nod. "All of you, vacate. Go into the café," he clarified.

As they quickly followed his command, he hurried along the corridor and eased through the doorway into the storeroom. He saw nothing, but he could hear the muffled sound of Laura crying.

Crouching, he made his way toward the sound, taking care to stay hidden behind the stacks of boxes. When he reached the end of the row, he carefully shifted a box until he could see the security guard. She looked cornered, as if she'd just realized she had gone the wrong way and was trapped.

If Laura wasn't involved, he would have charged her, but he had to try to deescalate. He stepped in front of her. "Give me the baby."

He'd startled her, and she tried to back away. She stumbled into a stack of boxes and, as she fell, Laura flew into the air. Adam dove, catching the baby in his arms and rolling his body to take the brunt of the fall with his shoulder, holding Laura safely above the ground.

The woman scrambled to her feet and ran out the way he'd come in.

Adam hated letting her get away, but he had his precious little football gal and that was what mattered. A sense of calm washed over him. She wasn't Chance, but Laura's warmth and sweet smile of recognition pushed back the darkness every bit as well as his therapy dog would have.

Tucking Laura under his arm, he headed back to the café. Mia broke away from the officer and ran to him, tears streaming down her face. "Mr. Adam. You saved her."

Adam bent to his knee and caught the little girl into his arms, holding her tightly as she rained kisses across Laura's face.

Adam searched over her shoulder to where he could see the cops with Isabelle. His heart plummeted as he realized she was still on the floor. He eased back from Mia. "I need to check on your mama."

"She's sleeping,"

Adam glanced down at Mia. "Is that what the policeman said?"

She nodded.

He stood, shifted Laura to his shoulder and grasped Mia's hand. He was not letting either of them out of his sight despite his compelling desire to check on Isabelle. "Okay, let's see if they woke her up yet."

Mia gazed up at him. "Maybe she's like Sleeping Beauty. She needs you to kiss her."

"Huh?" Adam swallowed hard.

"Like in the story. The prince kisses Sleeping Beauty and she wakes up."

Adam chuckled, trying to force humor through the sudden tightness in his throat.

"I thought I was a billy goat?"

Mia covered her mouth with both hands and glanced up at him with a deer-in-the-headlights look.

He smiled and gave her another hug. "I think I hear your mama's voice. I guess she woke up without me."

Isabelle stared with flickering vision into a sea of blurred, concerned faces and all she could think was that she was going to be sick. Who were all these people? Where was she? Squeezing her eyes shut, she tried to dig through the fog and remember. A nagging fear that she was forgetting something vital heightened the nausea. Panic pushed through the murkiness as memories of a hand snatching Laura filtered into her brain in a mosaic of confusion and anguish. She tried to raise her head to find the girls, but the world swam and a gentle hand on her shoulder kept her from sitting up.

"No," she protested. "I have to get up. I have to find my daughters." Even through the haze, she recognized the importance of what she'd acknowledged. In her heart, in every way that mattered, Laura was hers and she needed to save her.

"It's okay, Isabelle. I have them. The girls are safe."

Chills ran along Isabelle's spine and down her arms as Adam's reassuring voice penetrated her fog. Adam had her girls. Adam. Her heart filled to bursting with gratitude for this man who only days ago hadn't existed in her world.

She tried to push up again, wanting to thank him, needing to see the girls, but a wave of dizziness set her back. What had happened to her? What was wrong with this body she could no longer control?

The gentle hand was easing her down again. "Ma'am, please don't get up. We need to check you out. Get you to the hospital."

"No, my babies. I need to see Mia and Laura."

And then, suddenly, Adam was squatting beside her, one arm holding Laura in the football hold she'd taught him and the other wrapped around Mia. "We're right here, Isabelle. I have both girls safe. I won't let anything happen to them."

Isabelle let Adam's voice wash over her and tension eased from her body. She still felt awful and sick, but Adam's voice brought a measure of peace. Whatever had happened, the girls were safe with him.

She put up a futile resistance when the paramedic insisted she go to the hospital. She might have been able to stand her ground against him, but Adam's gentle plea that she do it to reassure Mia forced her surrender. She hated that Mia was witnessing this. If conceding that she needed medical evaluation could ease the fear on her daughter's face, that's what she would do. But with one caveat.

"You'll come?" she asked Adam.

"I will. I'm going to call Claire to meet us at the hospital, and then I will be right behind the ambulance."

When she woke, it was to an overwhelming sensation of dim lighting and a woman she presumed to be a nurse was sitting at a computer cart and typing on a keyboard.

"Ah, there you are. She's waking up, Doctor," the woman murmured.

An elderly gentleman approached her bed, speaking softly to her. "How are you feeling, Ms. Weaver?"

Isabelle blinked and considered how to answer. "Better than before, but I still feel like I got caught in a stampede."

He nodded sympathetically. "Can you tell me what happened?"

Isabelle didn't know exactly. She squeezed her eyes shut and tried to work her way back through the confusion. "The security guard. I think she put something in my coffee. I started to feel sick, and I asked her for help, but she took the baby." Panic swirled at the remembered terror. "Laura! Where is Laura?"

The nurse stroked her hand. "Don't you go worrying about those precious girls. That fine man of yours is taking quite good care of them."

Isabelle thought to argue, to tell the nurse that Adam wasn't her man, but she was too tired to fight what she wished were true. Adam was a fine man. And handsome too. She smiled, and when the nurse smiled back, Isabelle knew she was reinforcing the wrong impression. Sudden sadness swamped her. Adam wasn't hers and he never could be. A tear slipped down her cheek.

She brushed it away and lifted her gaze to the doctor. "Do you know what she gave me?"

He nodded. "We're waiting on final toxicology, but my guess is she gave you Rohypnol. You've heard of roofies?"

Isabelle nodded, relieved to realize she didn't feel quite so dizzy anymore. "How long before it wears off?"

"It's starting to. The paramedics reported that your coffee was knocked to the ground and there was a sizeable puddle. Presumably, you didn't ingest a full dose. We'll know more when the tox results arrive. Until then, you should just rest. Doctor's orders."

"Doctor's orders," Isabelle mumbled as she drifted back to sleep.

"When is Mama going to wake up?"

The dulcet tones of her daughter's voice drew Isabelle from slumber once more. Her eyelids fluttered, fighting back as she tried to open her eyes. She wanted to be awake, wanted to see her girls.

"I think Mama needs a Mia hug," Isabelle whispered.

"Mama!"

The sheer joy in her daughter's voice blew away the last vestiges of drowsiness. Isabelle raised herself on one stiff arm, wincing at the sudden shaft of pain. She must have bruised her elbow when she'd fallen. "Where's my best girl?"

Mia tried to climb her way onto the bed, but the guardrail made it difficult. Adam swooped her up in his arms and set her gently beside Isabelle. As her baby girl nestled into her side, Isabelle fought back tears. Nothing had ever felt as good as holding her daughter. For a moment, she closed her eyes and let herself simply be, breathing in the familiar scent of her daughter.

But even as she cherished the moment, her brain tormented her with questions.

Why was this happening and what would be next?

TEN

Adam glanced at his phone. He had a message from Nate, asking him to call. He excused himself. "I need to take this outside." He nodded to the security guard and strode to the window at the end of the hallway as he placed the call.

"Hey, Nate. What's up?"

"Anyone with you?"

"Negative. I'm at the end of the hallway. Why?"

"Fingerprint results are in."

"And?"

"They're not what I expected. I won't lie. It doesn't look good for Isabelle."

Something twisted deep within Adam's gut. "What aren't you telling me?"

"Nothing. I'm not jumping to conclusions until I interview her and see her reaction." He paused. "But, Adam, be careful. Isabelle may have been hoodwinked by her friend…or you and I have been played for fools."

Adam glanced back at Isabelle's room and a pain stabbed in the general vicinity of his heart. He forced a lid on his emotions and focused on the conversation.

"Are you coming to the hospital?"

"No. I want to do this in private. I spoke to the doctor. He's willing to release her. I'll arrange an escort."

"Where are we going?"

"Back to Claire's temporarily while we figure this out. If we need a safe house, we'll take it from there."

Adam disconnected the call. He had to get back to the room and prepare everyone to leave, but first he had to rein his emotions into control. For a long moment, he just stood staring out at the snowcapped mountains in the distance. He was trained to evaluate and not leap to conclusions. He needed to keep that same sense of open-mindedness now.

Given everything that had happened, the most reasonable conclusion was that Isabelle was an innocent victim. If Nate had evidence to the contrary, Adam would reevaluate. But even if she wasn't, his role had not changed. He was there to protect the innocent. The verdict might be out on Isabelle, but the children were blameless and deserving of his care—however temporary.

He fought off the thought of how the girls had wormed their way into his heart. His arm felt empty now when he wasn't bearing the weight of his precious little football.

Adam steeled his emotions and headed down the hallway to Isabelle's room. When he entered, Isabelle was preoccupied with the nurse giving her release instructions. She smiled up at him, seeming genuinely glad to see him. His heart gave a little lurch.

"They're letting me go home." Her face fell. "Well, not home, but wherever."

Despite his best instincts, Adam answered reassuringly. "Nate is sending an escort. They'll know where we're going."

She nodded in acquiescence, but he could see it was costing her. He shoved his own emotions away and reverted to warrior mode. His only task right now was to get them safely back to Claire's.

Nate buzzed Adam when the car was outside. He turned to Isabelle. "Time to go."

Her face was pale, and Adam realized that as happy as she was to be set free, she was apprehensive of leaving the safety of the hospital.

"It's okay," he promised. "Nate has you covered."

She nodded, and he fought the tug her brave expression had on his heart.

"We'll do this in stages. Claire and I will take the girls down. Once they're secure, I'll come back for you. The officer will remain on guard outside the door."

Once again, she nodded, though he noted she was careful not to move her head too quickly. "Still dizzy?"

"Some. The doctor said it was normal and will take a while to wear off."

"Okay. Rest here. I'll be right back."

He left without a backward glance and headed to the playroom where Claire had been entertaining the girls.

Mia saw him first and came running over. "Mr. Adam, I want to go home."

He crouched beside her. "How about we take a car ride back to Claire's and see Chance?"

"Will Mama come?" The thread of anxiety in her voice coiled inside him.

"She will," he reassured her. "She's feeling much better now."

He filled Claire in on the plan, and they all headed downstairs. Alert for anything even mildly threatening, Adam escorted them through the lobby to a side entrance. A dark SUV was waiting.

Adam rapped on the roof to get the driver's attention. The deputy popped the locks and came around to stand guard as Adam quickly settled the children inside. Once he'd gotten the girls harnessed into car seats, with Claire between them, he turned to the man. "Wait here. I'll be back with Isabelle."

The officer nodded his understanding, and Adam was just starting to close the door when alarms shattered the peaceful twilight and lights flashed in rhythm with the blaring sound.

Isabelle! Adam's first instinct was to send the driver on his way and head back inside to rescue her, but a flashback to the attack at the house changed his mind. If Laura was the true target, this was a distraction. He had to get the girls to safety.

He opened the passenger door and jumped in beside the surprised driver. "They won't be expecting me to come with you." He swiveled so he could see his sister. "Claire, where are you parked?"

"It was sleeting when I got here, so I opted to pay for indoor parking."

"Perfect." He turned to the deputy. "I want you to drive around to the ER entrance. Claire and I will take the children and head back inside. You drive around a few times and then head back to the station. Radio ahead to Nate so he can send other cars. Hopefully, whoever triggered this will follow you and we can lay a trap."

"Nate will have my head if I leave you," the deputy argued. "It's too risky."

Adam reconsidered his plan. It was hard to think with the blaring sirens. The noise and lights were triggering a panic attack, and he knew he could only hold it off for so long with all the sensory overload.

He pulled out his phone and quickly placed a call to Nate. Putting him on speaker, Adam explained the situation and then listened while the sheriff corroborated his plan. The deputy was clearly unhappy, and Adam made a mental note to discuss it with Nate later. For now, he had to escape.

They pulled up under the awning for the ER entrance and

Adam reversed his earlier procedure, unharnessing the girls. He handed Laura to Claire and turned for Mia, who stared at him wide-eyed. He wanted to take the time to comfort her, but that would have to come later. For now, he could only whisper a reassurance.

People streamed out of the hospital as the alarms continued to screech. Pulling Claire to the side, Adam edged their way around the crowd and headed inside. He squeezed his eyes against the blinding lights and tried to focus his attention on the people in his care. If he focused hard enough, he could turn the sirens into white noise in his mind.

"Adam." Claire tugged on his arm. "The parking garage is the other way."

"We're not going there."

"But you said—"

"Trust me. I have a plan."

He thought he heard her mutter, "Of course, you do," but there would be time for sibling payback later. Now he needed a vacant office. That proved easy to find. With everyone evacuating, the administrative offices were all empty. He walked down the corridor, looking for a room with windows. At the end of the hall, the conference room stood empty and dark. Heavy shades had been pulled across a wall of windows. Perfect.

Glancing over his shoulder to make sure no one had followed them, he ushered Claire into the room and closed the door behind them. He quickly scanned the area for the safest hiding spot. There was a bathroom at the rear of the room, conveniently adjacent to the windows. He lowered his voice as he spoke to Claire. "Lock yourself and the girls in there. I'm going for Isabelle."

She looked back at him and he could see the consternation in her eyes.

"Will you be okay?" Before he could answer, she glanced at Mia then continued in a soft voice, "You know what I mean."

He knew exactly what she meant. Before he'd turned himself into a recluse, Claire had witnessed the devastating impact of his PTSD too many times to count. He wouldn't lie to her.

"I'm fighting it the best I can. It will be better once we're away from the here."

Locking Claire and the girls in the bathroom left him with an uncomfortable memory of doing the same in the lawyer's office. Vowing that this time he would rescue them before any more danger came their way, he set off in search of Isabelle.

Blaring sirens and flashing lights compounded the nausea and dizziness that still plagued Isabelle, but they were nothing compared to her fear for Adam and her girls. She wanted to run after him, but the security guard had warned her to stay locked in the room. It was her safest option. She couldn't argue that, but it wasn't her own safety she was concerned about. Only a deep sense of knowing that Adam would come back for her kept her sheltering in place. He didn't need her complicating things.

The wait was interminable. Alarms continued to blare and she heard anxious voices as people evacuated the building. Second-guesses crowded her mind. Where were Adam and the girls? She needed to be with them. She should never have acquiesced to his plan. Worry plagued her. What had triggered the alarm? Was there a fire? Should she evacuate? Was she risking her life staying, or was it possible the people after her were behind this? Her anxiety had reached fever pitch by the time her phone dinged.

Isabelle almost collapsed in relief when she saw Adam's message.

I'm coming for you. Be ready.

Those six words settled her nerves momentarily, but it wasn't long before her thoughts were back in overdrive. If he was coming, where were the girls? Were they safe?

Isabelle began pacing the room. She chided herself for doubting Adam. He had been nothing but reliable. But as the alarms continued, another fear overtook her. What were all these lights and alarms doing to Adam? How was he coping? She'd learned enough from Daniel to know that sensory over-load was a dangerous trigger. He should have taken the girls and left. He should have—

A quick rap on the door interrupted her thoughts.

"Isabelle, open up. It's me."

On legs weak with relief, Isabelle stumbled to the door and flipped the safety latch. She'd never been so relieved as at the sight of Adam standing in her doorway. He pushed past her and closed the door.

"What's happening? Where are the girls?"

Adam gently grasped her arms to steady her. "They are safe with Claire. We're going to go get them as soon as I explain my plan."

Isabelle nodded and took a deep slow breath, trying to calm herself. "What's happening? Is it real…or is it them again?"

"I'm fairly confident it's them. The alarms began just as I was loading the girls into the car."

"Did you send them off?" Panic rose again at the thought of the girls being separated from her in a time of danger.

"No. I remembered how they set off the dogs in the ken-nel as a decoy while they went after Laura, so I hid the girls in the building instead. Nate's going to meet us."

"Okay." She offered him a wobbly smile. "I knew I could trust you to protect them."

A shadow flickered across Adam's face, but Isabelle didn't have time to root out the cause. Adam was heading to the door. He turned abruptly and she almost walked into him.

"Are you okay to do this? It might be too strenuous since you're still recovering."

"I'm a bit shaky, but I'll do whatever we need to do."

Adam's smile of approval gave her a needed adrenaline rush. He opened the door cautiously and scanned the hallway before leading her out. The fact that there was no sign of anyone coming for her indicated either this was a false alarm and really a hospital problem...or he'd been right about them going after Laura.

Adam took her hand and tugged her along behind him. He stopped at the corner and peered around to make sure no one was in the corridor. Once he was certain the way was clear, he pointed to the stairwell and told her to run.

"What about you?" She wasn't leaving him behind.

"Two steps behind you."

The sound of heavy footsteps running down the hall they'd just exited gave Isabelle a burst of energy. She and Adam shoved through the door into the stairwell and flattened themselves against the wall. Before long, they could hear men talking. Isabelle listened carefully, trying to catch what they were saying. The voices were too muffled to make out the words, but the angry, impatient tone was warning enough. These weren't hospital workers. She held her breath, half expecting them to burst through the doorway, and only released it slowly when the voices receded.

Adam grinned at her. "Let's go before they decide to come back," he breathed. At her nod, he took her arm and led her down the stairs. The steep concrete staircase exacerbated Isabelle's dizziness, making her extra grateful for Adam's support. As they finally approached the exit, he signaled her to wait while he eased open the door.

"No sign of anyone," he assured her. "I think all the action is in the front of the hospital." He pulled out his phone and texted Nate. After a minute, he glanced up at her. "Nate was waiting around the side so as to not draw attention. He'll pull around now. We need to be fast, and once we're in the car, I need you to crouch on the floor."

His thumb grazed her cheek as he gazed at her. "Are you up to that?"

Flutters of awareness confused Isabelle. She was relying on Adam to protect them. He wasn't supposed to make her have feelings she'd thought had died years ago. She forced herself to nod and speak. "You know I'll do whatever I need to for my girls."

His face broadened into a deep smile and he concurred. "I do. You've been absolutely amazing."

Her cheeks flushed at the compliment and Isabelle lowered her head. She wanted to tease him, say something to diffuse the sudden tension, but she was at a loss for words and could only manage a whisper. "Thank you."

The sound of Nate's car arriving saved her from any more conversation. She stood silently while Adam verified it was his friend. Once confirmed, he opened the car door so it was flush with the hospital exit. Keeping her head low, Isabelle dashed the short distance and crawled into the back of the vehicle. Adam climbed in behind her and closed the door.

"Did anyone see us?" he asked.

"Not that I saw," Nate replied. "Where's Claire?"

"Locked in a bathroom off the administrative offices."

Nate drove around to the front of the hospital and pulled up beside the police chief's car. "Wait here," he directed them. He was gone about five minutes before he returned with good news. "The building is secure. Adam, you can go get Claire and the girls. Isabelle, I think you should stay with me."

Isabelle wanted to protest, to tell him that she wanted to be the one to rescue her girls, but something in Nate's voice warned her not to argue. Adam headed into the building, and Isabelle uneasily observed Nate as they waited for Adam's return. Gone was the friendly man she knew from church. Tension radiated off him, and it set her nerves on edge. Something had changed and she had no idea what it was.

ELEVEN

Adam wanted to call it a successful day as the cars entered the drive to Claire's ranch. They'd survived the attack and had arrived safely, but his body still radiated tension knowing the most difficult part lay ahead.

Nate pulled his vehicle up to the house entrance. Adam and Claire, who had driven back in her car, went around to the garage. They parked the car and started up the path. Adam paused before they reached the house. Turning to his sister, he spoke in a low voice. "I know you need to see to the dogs, and I hate to ask more of you, but can you take Mia with you?"

Claire chuckled. "You really think Isabelle is letting Mia out of her sight?"

Adam closed his eyes a moment and breathed in deeply before letting his shoulders relax on a long exhale. "She won't have much choice. Nate needs to talk to her." He glanced over his shoulder to be sure they were alone. "Trust me, Mia shouldn't be within hearing distance."

Concern etched Claire's features, and she obviously had questions, but she simply bobbed her head in agreement. "Mia's wonderful with the dogs. It won't be a bother."

They reached the house just as Nate finished helping Isabelle and the girls from his car. "Hey, Mia," Claire called. "Want to come help me feed the dogs? I had a friend check on them, but I'm thinking they could use some love."

Mia turned her eager face to her mother. "Please, Mama."

Isabelle opened her mouth, and Adam was sure it was to veto the suggestion, but Nate stepped up beside her and spoke softly. Isabelle's expression grew grave. She gave a quick nod to Nate and then turned back to Claire and Mia. Only because he was watching so carefully did Adam pick up on her nervous tension.

"Go ahead, sweetie. I'm going to take Laura in for a bottle. But stay with Ms. Claire. Do whatever she tells you."

Mia took Claire's hand and skipped off to the kennels while Adam unlocked the front door. Chance was waiting as they entered. He bypassed Nate and Isabelle and leaned into Adam. Immediately, Adam felt his body lighten. He knelt and buried his face in the dog's soft fur. "I missed you, buddy." Chance burrowed hard against him. Adam laughed. "I guess you missed me too."

Isabelle set the diaper bag down on the sofa and faced Nate. "I need to make a bottle for Laura. I don't want to keep you waiting, but we stand a better chance of speaking uninterrupted if she has eaten."

"You seem to know her very well."

Isabelle didn't pick up on the edge that Adam recognized in Nate's words. She rifled through the bag in search of powdered formula and a bottle. When she found what she wanted, she looked up and shrugged. "I guess I do. Jess and I are both single moms. We were lucky we had each other to rely on."

"You were very close?"

"Like sisters," Isabelle replied sadly. "We chose each other to be family because we had no one." She turned on her heel and headed into the kitchen.

Adam followed. He opened the back door to let Chance out, then walked over to the counter. "I'll make coffee while you get the bottle ready." Thinking of her recent experience, he reconsidered. "Or would you prefer tea?"

She smiled tentatively. "Thanks. It's going to be a while before I can look at coffee the same."

Nate came into the kitchen and sat at the big farm table. Adam brought the coffee and Isabelle's tea over and settled down, facing the window. Claire's kitchen overlooked a vast nature preserve and, though he would have preferred to be hiking in it, just looking at the snow-covered pine trees soothed his soul. He sipped his coffee and waited for Isabelle.

Five minutes later, when she was still fussing at the counter, Adam knew she was stalling. Was it just nerves, postponing what she feared was bad news, or was she hiding something? Nate sat patiently, but Adam wanted to know the info his friend had withheld.

"Isabelle."

She looked at him, her expression as frightened as a cornered animal's. Adam pushed back his chair and went over to her. "There's no use postponing this." He angled his head toward the table. "Nate has results he needs to talk to you about."

She looked at him, fear in her eyes, and his chest tightened. "You know what it is?"

Was he overreacting? Or did the idea that he knew seem to trouble her more?

"I don't know it all, and we won't until we talk to you."

Her head lowered in resignation, Isabelle walked to the table and sat with Laura on her lap. She reached for the bottle before realizing she'd left it on the counter.

Adam picked it up and set it on the table. "Would you prefer me to feed her?" he asked gently.

She clutched the baby close to her chest, almost as if she could ward off bad news. "No." She shook her head. "I'll do it."

She lowered her head and appeared to be whispering a

prayer. Adam took his seat, facing her. After a minute, she looked up at Nate. "I'm ready."

Nate rested his palms on the table and leaned forward. "Isabelle, there's not any easy way to say this—"

"You found her body?"

"What?" Nate blinked. "No."

"Is that what you've been thinking?" Adam asked gently.

She nodded. "What else was I to think?"

Nate rubbed his eyes. "Not that."

Isabelle seemed to calm visibly at that news. "Then what is it?"

Nate caught her gaze and held it. "We got the fingerprint analysis back."

"Okay. Did it tell you who the men were?"

Nate shook his head.

Isabelle rolled her eyes. "Then what's the point of all this, if it didn't tell you anything—"

Nate broke in. "I didn't say it didn't tell us anything."

"Nate, please stop dancing around it. Just tell me what you found."

"We took fingerprints from Jess's house and more from the lawyer's office. We looked for a match but found only one. Presumably Jess's."

Isabelle mulled it over for a minute. "I guess that makes sense if she was in the lawyer's office to sign papers."

Nate nodded. "It would, except for one thing. The name they matched to was not Jess's."

Isabelle shook her head in confusion. "You've lost me."

"The fingerprints we took as elimination prints were from all the places in her home Jess might have touched. The kitchen, Laura's room, her bathroom. Those prints matched the ones found on a file and chair in the lawyer's office." Nate waited to see if she was following before he continued.

"They matched, but not to Jess. The fingerprints belong to a woman named Julia."

"That's not possible."

Nate turned over a paper that he'd placed on the table. "Is this Jess?"

Isabelle leaned forward, studied it, and then looked up at him. "You know it is. You've seen her at church with me every week."

Nate sighed deeply. "Isabelle, this woman's name is Julia. Her husband was a highly respected engineer for a military weaponry company. He was working on a top-secret project two years ago when he suddenly went missing. His wife, Julia, was considered a suspect in his disappearance. Three months after he disappeared, she went missing too. No one had any idea where she went until we got this fingerprint match."

Adam had been closely watching the exchange, noting Isabelle's stricken expression. Her hands were trembling as she set the bottle back on the table. He rose quickly and walked around to take Laura. She looked up at him in panic. "No, you can't have her."

Adam crouched beside her, putting a supporting arm beneath Laura. "I don't want you to drop the baby. Let me hold her while you explain to Nate."

She looked up at him, eyes wide, then turned to face Nate. "Explain? You think I knew this?" Her gaze swung wildly to Adam. "You too? You think I'm a part of this…" She gasped for breath and her body convulsed. "How could you, of all people, think that after everything we've gone through? They drugged me to get this baby. How could—" She pushed back the chair and, clasping Laura to her chest, bolted from the room.

Adam wanted to follow Isabelle, to reassure her that he had not thought any such thing, but the reality was, he hadn't been sure. Despite her reaction, he still wasn't. He looked at

Nate. The expression on his friend's face was bland, but Adam knew that beneath the quiet façade, Nate's brain was seething with the same questions, debating what to make of Isabelle's responses.

"I'm going to make some calls, see if I can find out more about this case." Nate paused and cleared his throat. "Can you reach out to your buddies, see if anyone has heard anything?"

Adam dropped his eyes as his chest tightened and apprehension darkened the edges of his vision. Reaching out to old comrades would be worse than tearing a bandage off a wound. It was more akin to ripping out the stitches that were holding him together.

Once he'd settled here in Colorado, he'd isolated himself from pretty much anyone in his military life, with the exception of Nate. When Adam had been drowning in a sea of undiagnosed symptoms, Nate had thrown him a lifeline, introducing him to the wilds of Colorado, to the healing power of nature. That meant Nate knew exactly what he was asking and thought it important enough to risk.

Adam walked over to the bay window and rested his palms against the cold glass as his mind sought solace from the forest. But his brain couldn't rest. He thought of Isabelle in the next room, the brave friend who was fiercely protecting a baby. The woman who, against his best instincts, had wormed her way into his life and maybe even his heart. To know the truth, for her, he would break his silence. "I'll make some calls."

Isabelle didn't know where to turn. The world was collapsing on her and she couldn't think straight. Jess wasn't Jess? Who was Julia? Had everything about this past year been a lie?

She sagged onto the bed. There had to be some explanation, some way to make sense of all of it. But she was so tired.

Her brain was still dulled from the effects of the drugging and she couldn't even figure out how to begin to process this news. All she wanted to do was to go to sleep and wake up to find it had all been a bad dream.

Laura started to squirm in her arms, and Isabelle knew she was sensing the tension. She held her close. "Don't you worry, my darling," she murmured as she gently stroked Laura's back. "I'm here for you. I won't let anyone hurt you."

But even as she made the promise, she knew it was impossible to keep. She had no way to do it on her own, and the two men who were her only help now doubted her.

It was too overwhelming. She'd coped with so much these past few years—Daniel's erratic behavior, his death, her despair, and her efforts to be a better mother to Mia. Just when it seemed she was going to make it as a single mother, this avalanche hit. It was too much. She couldn't do it alone.

You're not alone, her heart whispered. *God is always with you.*

She closed her eyes and tried to feel the truth in that, tried to find the words to pray. It was wrong to rely on her own strength. God had been good to her and He would continue to be if she remained faithful. But she was so very tired.

Isabelle laid Laura down on the bed and curled up beside her. She closed her eyes, intending to pray, but she could feel herself drifting off. Maybe just for a few minutes she would rest.

"Mama."

Isabelle fought her way through a cloud of sleep, drawn by the joyful sound of her daughter's voice. The sound of baby gurgles sang to her heart and she listened to Mia whispering to Laura as she played piggy toes with the baby's foot. Isabelle opened her eyes, intent on cherishing this precious moment of the three of them at peace together because she knew it wouldn't last.

Once Mia saw she was awake, she bounced up to grab a paper from the table. "Look, Mama. I made you a picture."

Isabelle took the drawing and smiled. Yet another tree. This was not Mia's norm. "You're getting really good at drawing trees, sweetie." She ran her finger along the smooth crayoned shape. "Is there a reason you're drawing so many?"

Mia's eyes welled up and her fingers rose to graze her necklace. Isabelle's heart cracked. "You're drawing them for Aunt Jess?" The name came out automatically before her brain caught up. But if she was confused, she certainly couldn't tell Mia she had the wrong name. Not now. Until she knew something for sure, her friend would remain Jess.

Mia hung her head and nodded. "It makes me feel close to her."

Isabelle wrapped her arms around her little girl, pulling her near. "It's okay to feel sad. I miss her too." She brushed her hand over the golden charm, remembering Jess giving the necklace to Mia. She'd had a matching one made for Laura. "Sisters of the heart," she'd said. Isabelle's heart tightened with the memory. They'd been so happy, widows both of them, yes, but grateful for each other and the precious children God had entrusted to them.

And now those children were solely her responsibility.

Isabelle gazed down at the tree drawing. She recalled telling Adam the story of how she and Jess had met, but the shortened version had left out so much—of their friendship, of the fragile bond of trust that had grown unbreakable. Until now.

Isabelle longed for those peace-filled days she and Mia had spent with Jess at Samaritan Home. She sighed softly, thinking of how Jess had shared her creative streak with Mia, how she had cultivated the little girl's love of art.

A memory surfaced of four-year-old Mia waving a paint-brush and splattering them all in green as Jess tried to include her in the painting of the mural. They'd joked that there had been more green paint on Mia than on the tree. Cleanup had…

Goose bumps rose along Isabelle's arm, multiplying until she was shivering with the force of the memory. The tree. Of course.

The tree holds all the answers.

That was the clue Jess had left and now, finally, she knew which tree Jess meant. It wasn't the Christmas tree, the one the men had tossed in their search for something. It was the tree she and Jess, with Mia's questionable help, had painted as part of a mural at Samaritan Home.

She had to tell Adam! Isabelle leapt from the bed, then had to stop and steady herself. These waves of dizziness that came with sudden movement might continue for a while, according to the doctor—a side effect of having been drugged. She shrugged the feeling off. She could tolerate a bout of dizziness if it meant she got some answers.

Answers.

The word drew her up short as she thought of Nate's revelation about Jess and the fingerprints. Did she really want those answers? Did she want the fragile memory of her friendship with Jess to be crushed beneath the weight of more revelations?

The pause gave other questions time to surface. How would Adam react to this news? The last time she'd spoken to him, she'd accused him of doubting her. Wouldn't this news only reinforce those doubts? Would he think she had been hiding this information until she'd had no choice but to reveal it?

Laura's happy gurgles broke through her devastating thoughts and brought her clarity. Whatever the truth was, she needed to know it, because this baby deserved a future and a mother. It didn't matter what Adam and Nate thought of her, she needed their help to solve the mystery of Jess's disappearance. If Samaritan Home held clues, then she needed to find them.

Adam set his phone aside. He'd left messages with as many of his former army buddies as he still had numbers for. Hopefully, between his unofficial inquiries and Nate's official ones, someone would know something. He was about to start researching Jess—he caught himself, Julia, and her husband, when he felt a presence behind him. He glanced up to see Isabelle standing in the doorway, looking hesitant. She had Laura in her arms and was holding Mia's hand. His heart gave a lurch at the portrait they portrayed—a small forlorn family.

Wanting to do something to cheer them up, he forced a smile. "I hope you liked Mia's drawing."

Isabelle nodded, but she seemed distracted, troubled. Unsurprising really.

"Is Claire in the house?"

"She's in the kitchen. Mia was giving her drawing lessons, but she was going to start lunch."

"I'm going to bring the girls there and get a bottle for Laura. Then can we talk?"

"I'll wait here."

The trio left as quietly as they'd entered. Adam resumed his internet search while he awaited her return. He found several news stories about the disappearances written at the time, but nothing much in the way of follow-ups. Had interest waned? Or had the stories been squashed?

He heard Isabelle walking back down the hall, but made no effort to hide what was on his screen. She didn't appear to notice immediately.

"I will apologize to Claire when I can do it without Mia

hearing, but I'm sorry. You two should not have to be caring for my daughter."

Her stilted, formal tone worried Adam. The news about Jess, his doubts, and her despair had cost them the easy camaraderie that had made the past few days manageable despite the stress. Seeking to regain that balance, he made a peace offering. "You've been through a tough time. It's okay that you needed to sleep. Claire doesn't mind."

"But the children are my responsi—"

He knew the moment her gaze landed on his screen.

"Is that about Jess?" She blinked. "I'm sorry. I can't think of her by any other name."

"This is about her husband, Robert. I've been trying to find any information that might help us figure out what it's all about."

"Have you? Found anything, I mean. About him or what he was doing?"

"Not yet." He decided against telling her of his phone inquiries.

"About the drawings Mia has been doing."

Adam blinked at the quick change in topic. "Yes."

"They gave me a clue."

She stopped, seemed hesitant, almost as if waiting for his approval to continue.

"Mia's drawing of a tree gave you a clue?"

She nodded. "Remember that odd message on my phone? 'The tree holds all the answers'?"

At his quick nod, she continued. "And remember I told you about Jess giving us a place to stay at Samaritan Home? What I didn't mention, because honestly it just didn't seem important, was that while we were staying there, Jess, Mia and I painted a mural on the community room wall."

Her gaze fell away and she fleetingly closed her eyes. "Mia

has been drawing that tree over and over as a way to stay close to her aunt. When she showed me the most recent one this afternoon, I was thinking…wondering how I could have been so wrong about Jess. I was remembering that day of us painting and suddenly it all made sense."

She hesitated a moment. "I know it looks bad, like I might have been hiding this all along. And I understand why you might think I knew." She leveled her gaze to meet his. "I promise you, I didn't. This is as much a shock to me as it is to you. More so really. Jess was my best friend and my support through a really difficult time in my life when I didn't know what I was doing or how to survive. To suddenly find out that none of that was real?"

She shuddered but continued. "I can't think about that now. I have two girls to protect from men who want something I don't understand." She pointed at the drawing. "This tree might hold the clue. But I'll understand if you're done with this. I'll find a way to do it on my own."

The words could have sounded pathetic, but her delivery was so strong, so intent, that Adam found himself believing her. Because he wanted to or because she was telling the truth? He didn't know. But he had to help. "Can we go there?"

"Yes. I can call the pastor and ask him to let me in. But what about the girls? I don't want to bring Mia back there, but leaving them here hasn't been safe."

"I'll arrange protection with Nate and Claire."

He could see the doubt creep into her face at the mention of Nate's name. "Isabelle, neither Nate nor I wanted to believe you were involved, but—"

"I get it. Neither of you knows me well enough to be sure I'm not. The thing is, I know I'm not, and I have someone after me, so I have to do something about it. At the moment, checking out the tree in the mural is the best lead I have."

TWELVE

Tears welled in Isabelle's eyes as Adam pulled Claire's truck into the parking lot behind Samaritan Home. He seemed to sense her mood and gave her time.

She climbed out of the car and just stood and stared at the building. There was so much emotion tied up in this building— recovering from Daniel's death, building a friendship and a new life with Jess and Laura.

She started to tremble.

Adam came up beside her and rested his arm around her shoulder. She wanted to lean into him, but at the same time, she was mortified. Explaining her reaction would mean baring too much of the wrecked person she had been.

"I'm sorry. It's just...hard."

He squeezed her shoulder in acknowledgment, but she knew he didn't understand the half of it. He'd think it was about what had happened with Jess, and that was a huge part of it. But it was so much more, and all of that was also tied up in Jess.

All the memories, how fragile she'd been, still reeling from Daniel's death and her inability to cope. She'd known she wasn't being a good mother to Mia. She'd been barely able to function as an adult, so lost in despair over the loss of her husband, so wrapped in grief that she hadn't been able to save him. How many nights had she tormented herself with guilt? She'd been on a dark road, unable to see her way clear, but she'd been trying to find a new life to share with Mia, determined to do better by her daughter. Jess had thrown her a lifeline.

No matter what the truth was, she would always be grateful for that. She would always owe Jess.

Something settled in her at that. She needed to be here, to search this place as repayment to Jess for her new life. It was the very least she could do.

"Let's go inside. The pastor said he had a meeting across town but would leave the door open for us."

Walking through the doorway and into the huge rec room was like stepping back in time, but Isabelle pushed forward. She had a task to accomplish, and she needed to do it as quickly as possible.

"The community room is up on the second floor." She confidently led the way through a maze of rooms and up a wide staircase that had seen better days. Several of the sagging steps creaked when she stepped on them. Had the building always been this decrepit, or had it just fallen into disrepair since she'd last been there?

She walked ahead of Adam down the hall and stopped in the arched doorway to just take a moment and absorb the sight.

Adam gave a low whistle. "You and Jess did this?"

"Mostly Jess, with Mia's help. My talents don't run to art."

The far wall was divided into two huge plate-glass windows with a long stretch of wall between them. On that wall, Jess had painted an enormous weeping willow tree. Isabelle smiled, remembering how she and Mia had watched it take shape. Mia had been absolutely enthralled.

Even now, almost a year later, the mural was so vivid that the tree seemed three-dimensional.

Dazed, Isabelle walked over to the wall and ran her fingers lightly over the painted surface. Memories crowded in.

Jess feathering the brush to create the leaf patterns. Mia joyfully splattering paint. Isabelle had mostly been responsible for cleaning up the mess.

Adam came up beside her. "Where do we start? Do you have any idea where she might have put something?"

Snapping herself out of the memories, Isabelle focused her attention on their mission. She shook her head in answer to Adam. "Jess certainly didn't do anything while we were working on it. Maybe she came back later when she had something to hide."

"In that case, we should be looking for a loose board or a hole." Adam knelt and felt around the roots of the tree. He pressed on the boards, seeking any sign something had been removed and replaced.

Isabelle tapped on the wall, hoping to hear a hollow sound. Was it possible that within this wall there was something of worth? Something that would explain this dangerous mess they were in?

Her tapping resulted in nothing. The sounds were all solid, but as she examined the tree closely, that sense of three-dimensionality nagged at her. In her recollection, the mural had been a flat surface. But there was no sign of construction, no indication this painting was anything other than what they had created. Doubt assailed her and she began to worry this had just been a fool's errand.

"Claire keeps a toolbox in the truck. I'm going to run down and see what's there. Will it be a problem if we have to pry off some boards?"

Isabelle shrugged. "I don't think so." She ran a finger along the window ledge and it came away covered in dust. It had clearly been a while since this room had been used.

Adam left, and Isabelle walked back to the tree. "Talk to me, Jess. What did you do here? Where are your secrets?"

She stroked her finger lovingly over the whimsical designs—the owl sitting on his branch, the delicate shading of the leaves, a rainbow of birds. Those had been Mia's request. They were so lifelike you could almost hear them warbling.

It was all so realistic, down to the knothole in the trunk.

A shiver ran down Isabelle's spine.

That knothole was new; it had not been part of the original design she and Jess had created.

Isabelle leaned in and studied the tree. Jess was so talented, Isabelle felt like she could feel the rasp of the bark as she touched the nooks and crannies. She grazed her knuckle along the seam in the wall that ran behind the tree limb. It was definitely raised, part of the design that gave the tree the dimension that had been nagging at her.

She tapped lightly on the knothole. The gnarled branches with their lacy leaves nearly hid the bright bluebird that sat perched in front of it, his beak pointing toward the hole, almost as if it were looking inside.

The bird seemed to call to Isabelle. She continued to trace the outline until she reached the dark hole at the center. Her finger did scrape along a rough edge then, right before it disappeared into the darkness.

Isabelle gasped and fell back, almost afraid to look. Gathering her courage, she leaned forward again to examine the knothole more closely. It wasn't a painting. It really was a hole carved into the tree. She took out her phone and used the flashlight to try to see inside. The light appeared to bounce off something reflective. Excitement skittered along her spine as she angled herself to see better, but the hole was too small to get her head into. She stepped back again, wanting a wider perspective before she thrust her hand into darkness.

Isabelle heard the creak of a stair tread. "Adam," she called, "I think I found something."

There was no reply and unease shivered through her. Thinking quickly, she made her way to the closet in the corner and opened it, pretending to look up on the shelf. If there was someone besides them in this house, she couldn't let them know what she'd found.

She listened carefully, but all was silent.

Maybe she was wrong. No one was there.

It was probably just her nerves.

She pulled out her phone and called Adam. "I think I found something. Do you have a good flashlight?"

"In the truck. I'll bring it in."

"Were you just back in the house?"

"No, why?"

"I thought I heard something."

"I'll look around, but there are no other cars here."

Despite his reassurances and her own eagerness to see what was in the hole, Isabelle waited by the closet until she heard Adam's footsteps and his voice calling out to her. "It's only me."

He walked into the room loaded with an ax, a hammer, chisel, pry bar, some loose rope, and an industrial-size flashlight. He set the items on the floor before handing her the flashlight.

Isabelle's eyes widened at the sight of the ax.

"I'm hoping not to need it, but we'll see. What did you find?"

She led him to the tree and took his hand, placing it on the bark. She told herself the flush of excitement was just anticipation of what they would find.

"See this bird? See where it's pointing?"

Adam ran his hand along the wall, following the bird's line of sight right until his hand disappeared into the wall.

"Whoa."

"I tried to use the flashlight on my phone, but I couldn't see far enough into it."

"Let's use the one I brought. See if you can angle it from above my head, so I can see."

Isabelle stood behind him and shone the light over Adam's shoulder as he tried to peer inside. When he couldn't see, he thrust his arm into the hole.

"There's something down there, but I can't reach it." He readjusted himself and leaned his whole body into the wall, reaching down as far as he could. "My fingers are scraping the top of something metal, but I can't get a grip on it."

"Jess must have had some way of getting it in there."

"She probably just dropped it in. I think we're going to have to open the wall."

Isabelle hesitated only a minute. "It could be a matter of life or death. Pastor Frank will understand."

Isabelle watched as Adam tapped along the wall below the knothole. The tapping rang hollow most of the way down, but a foot off the floor, the sound turned to more of a solid thump.

It was all Isabelle could do not to grab the claw and rip open the wall herself. What would they find inside? Jess's text had implied there would be answers.

Adam made a small hole then handed the chisel to Isabelle to hold as he used the pry bar to pull back the plasterboard.

"I've got it." He reached into the opening, pulled out a long silver cylinder, and handed it over to her. He stuck his hand back in the wall.

"I'll take that, thank you."

Startled by the voice, Isabelle turned around and found herself staring down the barrel of a gun.

She hadn't imagined it before. There *had* been someone in the building—someone who was waiting for them to find this clue. She couldn't give him the canister, not when it probably held all the answers to Jess and her secret life.

Adam rose to his feet behind her. Just feeling his strength at her back gave Isabelle courage. She slung the handle of the cylinder over her shoulder. "Why should I give it to you?"

The man laughed and waved the gun in her face. "This reason enough?"

Her bones turned to liquid. Mia and Laura's faces flashed before her eyes. Who would raise her babies if he killed her? But then she thought of Jess.

"Pretty convincing," she murmured, taking a step forward. She reached to take the strap from her shoulder and in one smooth movement, swung it forward with the full force of her body. She aimed the canister at his head but continued into the swing and brought the chisel down on the hand that was holding the gun, sending it flying. She'd hit him on the wrist and blood poured from the wound, but he charged at her. She turned and ran, but he quickly caught her and ripped the cylinder away.

From the corner of her eye, she saw Adam retrieve the gun. He called out. "Let her go. Now!"

The man didn't loosen his grip. Adam fired. His impeccable aim sent a bullet through the man's knee.

With a howl, the man dropped to the ground.

Isabelle stepped up to him. "I'll just take that back now." She snatched the cylinder. He tried to lunge at her again, but his leg gave out.

Adam quickly tackled him and pulled his hands behind his back. "Hand me that rope."

Isabelle brought it and Adam quickly hogtied the gunman. "Who are you working for?"

The man was obviously in pain, but the look that settled over his face was a mix of fear and determination. He reminded Isabelle of the man they'd apprehended in the kidnapping attempt. He wasn't saying anything.

Adam shrugged. "Have it your way." He pulled out his phone and called Nate. There was no answer, so he called dispatch instead. When he finished, the man laughed crudely. "They'll never get here in time."

Adam ignored him. He picked up the ax and swung it into the wall, then stretched in and pulled out a backpack. He reached for Isabelle's hand. "We shouldn't wait around."

Adam didn't let it show, but the man's words troubled him. He sounded too confident. He and Isabelle started down the stairs, but the sound of cars arriving stopped him. "That's too soon to be cops. Is there another way out of here?"

Isabelle's face had drained of color and she was leaning against the wall. She nodded weakly. "I need a minute."

"I don't think we have one."

"Okay." She blinked, gathered her strength and pushed away from the wall. "We need to go up. There's a back staircase, but we can only get to it from the top floor."

"Can you do it?"

She faced him calmly. "I have no choice. Follow me."

Adam let her lead, but he stayed close behind, ready to catch her if she fell. He'd underestimated her, though. Isabelle's resolve was as strong as any soldier's he'd ever served with. She may have looked on the verge of collapse minutes ago, but she charged up the stairs as if she'd trained for it her whole life.

They were halfway up the last flight when the front door slammed open. Footsteps pounded in the foyer and angry voices rang out. Adam wished he'd taken the time to gag the man they'd tied up when he heard him calling out to his buddies. He could hear the men charging up the stairs and knew they were running out of time.

Isabelle had reached the landing and she signaled to him to follow her. Ignoring the open door straight ahead, she stealthily led him down the hallway and through a maze of rooms. Adam could hear shouts from below as they started up the staircase. It sounded like there were at least four pursuers, so they would fan out and search the rooms quickly.

Isabelle didn't seem fazed. She opened a door, cringing at the squeak, and guided him through. Once she'd closed it, she whispered, "Do you want to escape or try to trap them?"

Adam almost laughed. She was amazing—so bold and confident.

"I want to trap them, but we're outnumbered and I'm sure they're heavily armed. We need to get back to the girls."

He didn't want to say anything to alarm her, but the fact that they'd been so easily tracked worried him.

Isabelle hadn't been on these stairs in over a year. The last time had been when she'd played hide-and-seek with Mia. She had to think of this escape the same way—and ignore the deadly consequences of losing.

She pulled out a piece of rope she'd stuffed in her pocket and tied the door handle shut. It wouldn't stop the men, but it might buy some time. She quickly led Adam down the stairs. Because this house had been used for a variety of purposes over the years, most of the old features had been left intact. She'd been told the top floor had once been servants' quarters, which was why the staircase exited in the basement kitchen. These days that kitchen was only used for parish events. Hopefully, no one would think to look for them there.

Above her, she could hear doors slamming as the men searched. Part of her wanted to crawl into one of the closets and just hole up, but survival instincts ran strong when she thought of the beloved children waiting back at Claire's.

When they reached the basement, she stopped and explained the layout. The door ahead lead into the open cafeteria-style room. At the far end of the hall was a small industrial-style kitchen. The door from there led into the parking lot where they'd left the truck.

"The danger is that there is no way to know if anyone is

on the other side until we open the door. But if the room is empty, it will be easy for us to get to the parking lot."

Adam nodded. "They haven't broken through upstairs yet, so let's just stand and listen for a minute."

Adam put his ear to the door, carefully listening for any sound. "I think we're clear—"

Pounding on the door above interrupted him.

"I wonder how long the rope will hold them back."

A resounding crash of the door hitting the wall answered that. Footsteps thumped down the stairs. Isabelle looked to Adam. "I guess we're taking a chance on the cafeteria."

"Let me go first. You wait behind the door. If it seems clear, I'll go right and you go left. We'll meet across the room."

Isabelle agreed. She waited for him to reach for the door and then stepped behind it. He turned the knob and jumped to the side as she took it from him, pulling the door wide. She held her breath, waiting to see his reaction.

"All clear," he breathed as he ducked into the doorway and ran the perimeter of the room, hugging the wall.

With the sound of the men growing closer, Isabelle didn't waste any time. She ducked around the door and started to the left. Spying a rack of chairs, she pulled it in front of the door, hoping to buy time again. Once it was wedged in place, she took off toward the kitchen, where Adam was waiting for her. The kitchen door had a window, so she pulled back the curtain to check the parking lot. Her heart sank.

Adam was looking over her shoulder, so she felt the moment he noticed. All the tires on Claire's truck had been slashed.

Isabelle's spirits sank. Behind her, she could hear the shouts of the men in pursuit. Ahead lay a parking lot with the disabled truck. They were trapped.

THIRTEEN

"Come on." Adam opened the kitchen door, grasped Isabelle's hand, and dashed for the truck.

"What are you doing?" Isabelle asked as he opened the passenger side and helped her in. He ran around to the driver's side and climbed in before answering.

"We're sitting ducks if we wait here."

"But the tires."

"Won't be the first time I've driven on rims." Adam gripped the steering wheel and glanced over at her. "Make sure you're buckled in and hang tight. It's going to be bumpy." The church was on the outskirts of town, so he took a sharp right out of the parking lot and headed for the sheriff's station. He eyed sparks shooting out from the wheel rims and could only pray nothing ignited before he could get to help. But that wasn't the most frightening sight in his rearview mirror. A large SUV, with the advantage of four intact wheels, was bearing down on them. Adam pressed down on the accelerator and the truck shuddered. The wheel in the back was dragging and it was all he could do to keep them on the road.

"Call Dispatch. Tell them we're headed in town, but have a tail. Ask them to send extra backup."

Before Isabelle could make the call, a wail of sirens pierced the air with ear-shattering relief. Adam waved the lead car on and pulled to the side of the road as the second car whipped past.

Behind him, Adam could see the vehicle tailing him swing in a wide circle and take off in the opposite direction, a sheriff's SUV in pursuit. Relief poured through him. Driving this truck had felt like being back in combat. He fought the encroaching memories, trying to hang on to his focus and keep the attack at bay.

Beside him, Isabelle was trembling. Pushing his own torments aside, he reached for her hand. "It's okay. We're safe now."

She swallowed and nodded quickly. "I know. I'll be fine in a minute. But I need to get back to the girls. Make sure they're okay too."

Adam pulled out his phone to see if he'd gotten any response from Nate yet. Nothing. He didn't think the sheriff had been in either of the vehicles that had passed them, so he called again. This time Nate picked up.

"Almost there," Nate said. "I sent the other cars after them, but I'll come for you."

Just as promised, Adam saw the familiar sheriff's vehicle make the turn five hundred yards ahead. He waved Nate down. The sheriff hopped out and rushed to Isabelle's side of the truck. "You guys all right?"

Isabelle rolled the window down. "We're fine now that you're here."

"What happened?"

Isabelle started to speak, but Adam interrupted her. "Where are Claire and the girls?"

"Under guard back at the house, where you left them."

Adam inhaled deeply and let it out in a rush in an attempt to draw in some energy. "Why didn't you answer when I called?"

"I was interviewing a prisoner."

Adam just nodded and let his head fall forward.

"What can you tell me? Who should my deputies be looking for?"

Isabelle answered. "They must have tailed us from Claire's. I thought I heard a sound while Adam was outside getting tools to break open the walls, but Adam didn't hear or see anything, so I figured it was just nerves. It wasn't. Apparently, the man was waiting to see what we found before trying to take it from us."

Adam lifted his head and laughed at that. The adrenaline rush was finally fading and laughter felt like welcome relief. He grinned at Nate. "You don't ever want to cross her. She swung a tube at his head and then gouged his hand with a chisel."

Nate ignored him and got right to the point "So, you found something? What?"

"We don't know yet. There was this cylinder the man tried to steal, and then there was a knapsack Adam grabbed at the last minute. We haven't had time to open either one yet."

"Can you give us a ride?" Adam asked. "We can look at everything once we get there."

"Sure thing. Let me just radio ahead to my deputies."

Isabelle climbed into the back of Nate's car, leaving Adam to sit beside his friend. Once Nate had called in an update, they headed to Claire's. They'd been driving for about fifteen minutes with Nate filling him in on his renewed frustration at the silence of their prisoner. "Someone is holding something over him, or he's scared, because he's not talking."

"Hopefully, we'll find something in Jess's papers to give us a clue."

"Does the nickname Silver Wolf mean anything to either of you?" Isabelle's voice sounded intrigued.

Adam swung his head around to her. "Why?" He could see

that she had opened the backpack and was going through the contents. Annoyance tugged at him. He had no authority to tell Isabelle she couldn't look through her friend's belongings, but instinctively he'd wanted to be observing when she did.

She held up a brown notebook that looked like a soft-covered journal. "Apparently, Jess had been keeping notes on her investigation in this journal. His name is mentioned on one of the last pages, from about a week before she vanished."

"The name doesn't ring a bell to me," Adam answered. "Nate?"

Nate's mouth was drawn in a tight line and his expression was grim. "I've heard the name. What does she say about him?"

"She seems to think he's behind her husband's disappearance."

"I thought she was blamed for that." Adam knew his phrasing was a mistake as he observed Isabelle. Her brows drew together and her eyes took on a combative glint.

"What happened to innocent until proven guilty?"

Her tone challenged him more than even the words did, and Adam knew he was treading in dangerous territory. "Let me rephrase. If she is looking at someone else to blame, it would appear she was not behind her husband's disappearance, but is there anything in that notebook to indicate she had information about it? Knew he was planning to disappear?"

The tension that had held Isabelle like a coiled spring eased and her shoulders dropped. "No. Her first notes seem to be fearful, then angry at him—like she had discovered something. I'll have to read more closely. I was just scanning for anything that would jump out at me. This name did."

"Why don't you message some of our ranger buddies and see if they have any intel?" Nate suggested. "If this somehow involved the military, some of them might be more in touch than either of us still is."

Adam opened his phone and composed a message to the same former members of his unit that he'd contacted earlier. When he was done, he looked back at Isabelle. She still had her head bent over the notebook, but he noticed her rubbing her forehead.

"Dizzy?"

She looked up, her forehead drawn tight. He could see the fatigue radiating off her. She nodded and then winced at the movement. "Yeah, I've never been good at reading in the car under the best of circumstances."

"Set it aside," he said softly. "There will be time to look when we get back to Claire's. Why don't you close your eyes and rest until we get there?"

Her glance revealed her disquiet. "Because it feels like I'm wasting precious time that might cost Jess her life."

Adam startled himself with the strength of his reaction to her words, the yearning to comfort her. He'd long since resigned himself to the life of a bachelor. He had nothing to offer Isabelle—and even an offer of comfort was likely unwelcomed when coming from him. It had been only hours ago that he'd effectively accused her of criminal activity.

Adam sighed inwardly and faced forward. Isabelle was quite capable of surviving without him.

Nate's radio crackled, interrupting his musings.

"We lost them, boss."

Adam didn't recognize the voice, but it was clearly one of the deputies.

"Where did you lose them?"

"Out by Five Corners." The man's voice sounded baffled for a moment. "We were hanging tight on their tail and they just vanished—like some spaceship just spirited them away."

Adam watched Nate roll his eyes. "Well then, retrace your steps and find that portal."

Adam laughed out loud as Nate closed the connection. Nate shook his head. "My sci-fi rookie. He's got good instincts, though, so I ignore the woo-woo stuff. Let me check with the other car."

Adam stared out the window as Nate connected with his other deputy. When that driver also reported losing them in the blink of an eye, Adam's spidey senses started tingling. He checked his phone and was surprised to see it lit with responses. He scrolled down and the news got worse with each one.

"Uh-oh."

"What?" There was a thread of fear in Isabelle's voice, and he had the passing thought that this time it was justified. He glanced at Nate before answering.

"Quite a few of my buddies recognized the name. I have to call for more details, but it's clear. Silver Wolf is bad news. Really bad news."

Isabelle tried to continue reading, but the winding mountain road was making her dizzy and she was being distracted by the bits of conversation she could overhear. When Adam finally disconnected the call, he angled himself so she could see his face as he spoke.

"I'm not going to underplay this. The news is bad."

He looked at Nate. "Silver Wolf is an alias for Alexander Michael James III."

Nate made a groaning sound that twisted Isabelle's gut. "Who is he?"

"Short version, he's former military. He was dishonorably discharged for his rogue behavior. Last my friend knew, he'd headed up a band of ruthless mercenaries. That's when he picked up the name Silver Wolf."

Isabelle's blood went cold but she forced herself to speak calmly. "Why does he want Laura?"

Adam hesitated before answering. "I don't know yet. At a guess, I'd say it has something to do with her father's disappearance. Hopefully, we'll find out more when we get into the stuff Jess hid." He turned to Nate. "That explains why the men we've captured won't talk. We need to find a safe house pronto."

Nate's phone started to ring. "It's Claire. Can you get it? The road up ahead washed out in the storm and repairs aren't finished. I need to focus on driving."

Before Adam could answer, a gunshot ricocheted off the hood of the patrol car, quickly followed by a barrage of shots that showered down around them.

"Isabelle, get below window level," Nate ordered.

"What about you and Adam?"

There was a moment of silence as the two men locked eyes. A chill ran through Isabelle. She was seeing them transform into warrior mode.

"We've been through this before," Adam finally admitted, his rough voice confirming her suspicions.

"We recently upgraded the vehicles," Nate interjected. "This one has the latest protection, but I'll be less distracted if I know you are out of the line of fire."

His attempt at reassurance fell flat. Isabelle wanted to protest that they wouldn't even be in this situation were it not for her, but she knew that would carry little weight. These men were born protectors. It was in their blood, and they were highly trained. Trying to argue would only distract them. She could help most by staying out of their way. And praying.

Nate got on the radio to call for backup while Adam scanned the mountainside, trying to locate their adversary. He tossed her his phone. "Text Claire. Tell her we're in a spot of trouble but to stay secure and we'll be there as soon as possible."

Isabelle could barely hold the phone with her trembling hands, but she forced her fingers to type out the message. She couldn't help herself from adding *I'm sorry* at the end. This was all her fault.

Well, no, it was Jess's fault. But actually, the blame was all on the mercenary, on Silver Wolf. The phone pinged and Isabelle read Claire's reply. "She has both girls and is barricaded in the surgery at the kennel."

Isabelle offered prayers for Claire, the children and the dogs. *Please, Lord, keep Claire and the children safe and don't let any of Claire's rescues be harmed in this fight.*

Nate's tense voice broke through her prayer. "What do you see up ahead?"

Adam pointed. "See that glint? I think they're up there."

"Notice how no other cars have come by in the opposite direction? I'm guessing they've barricaded the road up ahead. They're not letting us through alive."

Adam agreed, and Isabelle's heart skipped a beat at his calm revelation. How could they speak of this so matter-of-factly? They were on a strip of highway that cut through the mountains. One side was dense forest. The other dropped off sharply into a deep ravine. There was no way out but forward through this trap.

"They made a tactical error revealing too soon, though," Adam murmured.

"Agreed. That overlook up ahead—360 and reverse?" Nate suggested.

"Can you go in full speed and still pull out in time?"

"No, but I can make it look like I'm going to."

Isabelle swallowed her gasp. She'd driven this road often enough to know exactly which overlook Nate was referring to. The road gradually sloped up before curving and heading back down the mountain. At the curve there was a dramatic overlook. She'd always wanted to stop and take in the view over the valley, but she'd never had the courage to get out of the car with Mia in such a precarious location. And now Nate was going to risk a life-or-death maneuver in that very narrow spot.

Dear Lord, help us. She bowed her head to pray, murmuring the prayers of her childhood because she couldn't come up with words on her own. She was beyond coherent thought because, if she allowed herself to think, she would burst into tears at the idea of her daughter and Laura alone in the world.

Dear Lord, protect my babies. Keep them safe from harm Protect us from all evil.

Over and over, she repeated the prayers as the car continued to climb under a relentless barrage. Bullets pinged off the doors and roof, but Isabelle sensed that Nate was ignoring them. Bullets were the least of their concerns. The most treacherous stretch was just ahead, and if the mercenaries had their way, they would never make it off the mountain alive.

FOURTEEN

"Pray, Isabelle. Like you've never prayed before."

With those words, Nate braked hard and began to swing the car into a tight arc. Adam braced himself as the tires skidded on gravel and rocks shot up at the underside of the vehicle. He ducked and pulled his jacket up to shield his head as a large chunk shattered the passenger window already weakened by gunfire. Glass showered down around him, the shards needling into his skin.

He held his breath as the car scraped the barrier, all but hanging on two wheels as Nate quickly accelerated out of the turn and roared off down the road they'd come.

Gunfire continued to pepper the vehicle. Nate's white-knuckled grip on the wheel was the only sign of the strain he was under. They passed no other cars on the way, which concerned Adam. Was there a barricade at this end too?

Nate was clearly thinking the same thing as he warned, "Isabelle, stay down. I don't think we're through yet. You should get down too," he directed Adam. "I'm wearing a vest."

"That won't save your head," Adam replied. No way was he leaving his friend to deal on his own while he took shelter.

They flew down the mountain, going airborne each time they hit a dip in the road. Adam knew it had to be rough on

Isabelle, especially with her residual dizziness, but she uttered no complaint.

As the slope of the mountain eased, they rounded a curve and found the roadblock stretching across both lanes with armed men on either side.

"This is where we find out how well the new safety designs hold up," Nate muttered as he floored the accelerator. At the last moment, Adam lifted the backpack to shield them from any attack through the broken window.

The car barreled through the barricade, bullets flying at them from both sides. Nate didn't slow down until they were out of range. "Everyone okay?" he asked as the bullet-ridden vehicle coasted to a stop.

Isabelle lifted her head warily. "Is it safe to get up?"

"For the time being," Nate answered.

"You're bleeding," she cried out as she hoisted herself onto the seat where she could see Adam.

"It's just from glass shards. Nothing serious. Nate's fine too. New vehicle held up pretty well."

Nate chuckled grimly. "Don't want to think about the repair bill, but it's still running. If everyone's okay, I'm going to start up again. Somebody check on Claire. We're going to have to take the back route to her ranch, and that'll cost us time."

The atmosphere in the car dimmed as they were reminded that though they'd survived this attack, the mercenaries weren't giving up.

Adam leaned back in the seat so he could see Isabelle. "How are you holding up?"

She smiled bravely. "Okay. I said a lot of prayers," she admitted.

"You have a strong trust in God."

"How can you not? Look at the impossible situation he just got us out of."

"I guess my driving gets no credit," Nate joked.

Isabelle wasn't offended. She knew Nate's faith was strong. "God gave you skills."

"That He did," Adam concurred. "This isn't the first time Nate's done the impossible to save me." The minute the words left his mouth, he wished he could recall them. The last thing he wanted to do was to open himself to questions.

As usual, Isabelle seemed to have an intuitive understanding. She changed the topic. "So, Nate, how are you going to get us home in time to rescue the girls and Claire?"

"With your prayers and my driving skills, Isabelle."

Adam glanced at his friend, knowing he was deliberately making light of a terrifying situation. With the road blocked, they were forced at least twenty minutes out of their way. A lot could happen in twenty minutes.

"Did anyone check on Claire?" Nate asked.

Isabelle retrieved Adam's phone from the floor of the car and handed it to him. He tried calling, but the phone rang through to voice mail.

The silence made him uneasy. Claire would know that they'd be worried. She wouldn't go silent without a reason. He could only hope the reason was that Nate's deputies had gotten there to rescue them and she was busy with the girls.

Doubt gnawed at him, though it was pointless to second-guess himself about leaving the girls behind with Claire. Nate had assigned a top deputy, former military like themselves.

Suddenly his blood ran cold. Former military. Suspicions spun through his brain. "Nate, what division was Deputy Stevens in?"

Nate glanced over and Adam could see he was trying to follow the train of thought without giving anything away. Adam continued. "Is Deputy Warren also headed to Claire's?"

Nate gave a slight nod, showing he'd clued in. "Yes. Let me have them check in."

Nate radioed both men. Deputy Stevens responded first.

"Have you made it to Claire's animal shelter yet?"

"Negative that. I must have run over some glass. Tire went flat. Changing it now."

"Deputy Warren?" Nate called into the radio.

"Roger. Not there yet, sir. Approaching. Over."

"I'm calling for backup. Let me know what you find when you get there."

The radio had no sooner gone dead than Nate's phone buzzed. Nate pulled it from its holster and tossed it to Adam.

"It's Deputy Warren."

"Answer and put him on speaker." Nate made sure the radio was off, and Adam set the phone on the center console.

"Sheriff Brant here. You're on speaker, Deputy."

"Radio off, sir?"

"Affirmative."

"Don't know how to say this without seeming a snitch, sir."

"Spit it out, Deputy."

"Deputy Stevens does not have a flat tire. I parked on the back road, intending to approach from the opposite direction. He is standing at the house, talking to a man who is holding the baby. He's got a gun pointed at your friend and a young girl."

Isabelle's muffled cry pierced the deadly silence in the car.

"Talking as in negotiating, Deputy?"

"Talking as in laughing like old drinking buddies. Wait. Now he's walking with the man toward a car." His voice lowered suddenly. "He's forcing the woman and the two children into the back seat."

"Did Deputy Stevens get in the car with them?"

There was an audible hesitation before Warren spoke. "No, sir. He picked up something from the ground and sliced his tire."

"Which way did the car go, Deputy?"

"Headed down the river road. Toward the cliffs."

"I'll call highway patrol. Thank you, Deputy. Your courage is appreciated. What was the car, color and make?"

The deputy had already disconnected, so Nate asked Adam to redial. It went straight to voice mail. Nate tried the radio instead. At first there was nothing but static. As seconds ticked by, a weak voice came through.

"Canyon Road. Silver SUV. They have subjects."

A gunshot exploded and the radio went silent.

No one in the car dared to breathe for a long moment.

"Thoughts?" Adam finally asked.

Nate replied. "Not good. That wasn't Deputy Warren."

He quickly put out an alert for backup from the next county and to Colorado State Patrol.

The silence hung heavily.

"One of my deputies is bad, and I can't be sure which one."

"Stevens served under Alexander James," Adam reminded him.

Nate nodded, and Adam waited. He had his own ideas, but Nate knew his men better.

"Serving with him makes him look guilty if we jump to conclusions." He paused, clearly unwilling to jump to those conclusions, and again Adam waited for him to process his thoughts.

"Serving under him might also mean he knows why not to join him if he was as rogue as you reported."

Isabelle interrupted them. "How much farther, Nate?"

Adam could hear the tension threading through her words. She must be barely holding panic at bay, and he had to give her credit. Over and over, she had showed mental fortitude worthy of a warrior.

"Too far," Nate muttered.

"But if they are really on Canyon Road, and we're on Canyon Road headed toward them?"

"Then maybe your prayers are answered, Isabelle. Maybe. But I don't have time to get backup here, so we'll have to figure it out on our own. Best estimate, we have ten minutes, fifteen tops, before they reach us. That's if they don't turn off somewhere along the way."

As Nate was talking, Adam was quickly mapping the road and distance in his head.

"We need to set up a roadblock. If you slow down, that will give us more time and we'll be able to see what we can use. The storm that washed out the road has to have knocked some trees down. If we can pull one into the road and make it look natural, it will give us an advantage."

Adam could feel Nate's lack of enthusiasm. "You have a better idea?"

"No. It's a good plan. I just don't like having to rely on the chance we will find something."

"It's not that much of a long shot. I hike these woods. There are a lot of downed trees. We should be able to see something. Isabelle, I'll look to the front and right if you could search the left."

Isabelle was happy to have something to focus on other than her terror about Mia, Laura and Claire being in the hands of a maniacal mercenary's man. She locked her desperate thoughts away and focused her attention on the forest streaming past the window.

After five tense minutes of visually scouring the side of the road, Adam spoke up. "I see one up ahead, but I'm not sure it's big enough. If we don't see something else soon, though, we'll have to come back and make it work."

Isabelle glanced at the tree he was talking about, but she

wasn't impressed. The kidnapper would easily be able to drive around it if they placed it to look natural, but if they added to it, the man was sure to realize it was a trap. She didn't want to consider what he would do then.

The minutes ticked by with pressure mounting as they continued to evaluate the trees.

"I think we need to admit defeat and make do with the one I saw," Adam conceded. "We need time to set it up, and we're running low."

Nate agreed. "We need time to hide the car too."

"I was thinking about that. Why don't you and I stay behind to create an ambush. Isabelle can drive the car out of sight."

This wasn't the time to pick a fight, but Isabelle knew she could not leave when her daughter's life was at stake. "Wait," she called as Nate started to make a U-turn. "I see something up ahead that looks like roots in the air."

Adam turned to look in the direction she indicated. "Bingo! That's perfect." He had the door open and was out of the car before Nate even pulled to a full stop. He ran over to assess the tree and quickly signaled approval.

Working together, they grasped the roots and began to pull the tree across the road, arranging it to look as natural as possible. The tree was massive, and it was a struggle that left them covered with mud and leaves, but the tradeoff was that it provided enough cover for Nate and Adam to hide in the branches to wait for the kidnapper.

Adam rubbed his hands on his pants and faced her. "I know you don't want to do this, Isabelle, but we need you to take the car and drive back along the road. Block traffic so no one else can come by."

Isabelle bit her tongue and walked back to the car.

Adam followed her to the vehicle. "I left the gun in the glove compartment. Would you know how to use it?"

She shrugged. "Not really. If I see anyone coming, I'll hide in the forest." She climbed in and put the key in the ignition before turning to him. "I don't like this, but I trust you to protect Mia and Laura and Claire. Just don't do anything that will get you hurt."

The last words were the hardest thing to say, but she had to do this for him. She had to know that she was not putting pressure on him.

He stepped up to the patrol car's window and leaned in. "We will rescue them because this is what we are trained to do. Trust me."

Eyes brimming, Isabelle could only nod. "I do," she whispered. "I absolutely do."

Adam bent forward and kissed her cheek before stepping back. "Go," he uttered. "I'll call when it's safe."

Isabelle reversed and turned the vehicle around. For a moment, she almost considered obeying. The tears pouring down her cheeks were not only testament to her faith in Adam, but also because her heart was petrified of losing him. How could he expect her to just wait in safety with so many lives in danger?

Isabelle knew the answer to that. He expected her to stay safe so he didn't have to worry about her. Well, he wouldn't have to worry about what he didn't know.

But she knew he also had made the request because he and Nate needed to be certain of their surroundings. If she suddenly appeared back at the roadblock, she could interfere with their strategy.

Isabelle tried to comply. She drove back the way they'd come until she passed a curve that took her out of view. The road was straight far enough ahead that she could park sideways in the middle of it to create a roadblock without fear of someone accidentally hitting the car.

She tried to sit and wait.

She prayed for their safety.

She prayed for the success of their plan.

She prayed for them to capture the kidnappers and free Mia, Laura and Claire.

And then she couldn't stand it a moment longer.

She opened the driver's door, grabbed the keys from the ignition, and jumped out onto the road.

She wouldn't risk ruining their plan, but there was no reason she couldn't hike back through the woods as long as she stayed hidden deep enough in the forest. And if she walked parallel to the road, she wouldn't risk getting lost.

Her mind made up, Isabelle set off through the forest.

The going was harder than she'd expected. Snow began falling again as she trudged through the heavily wooded area. She was grateful for the difficulty of walking because it helped keep her mind from giving in to the absolute terror that threatened whenever she thought of her precious daughter in the clutches of a kidnapper. Pain wrenched through her body at the thought, but she used it as inspiration to keep moving despite frozen feet and snow blowing in her face. She couldn't hear anything, and her imagination ran wild.

Maybe she should have stayed back at the car.

FIFTEEN

Isabelle eased her way through the forest until she could see the roadblock. Within minutes, the sound of an engine alerted her to a silver SUV approaching the ambush site. She buried her face in her hands, peering between her fingers and the branches, praying with all her might that Claire and the girls were safe. She saw no sign of Adam or Nate, but presumed they were waiting for the right moment to strike.

Heart in her throat, Isabelle watched the driver pull to a stop at the downed tree. He got out and walked over to it, his body language revealing his frustration even though she couldn't make out the words he was yelling. She watched with bated breath as he searched the area. It made sense that a trained mercenary would be wary of a trap. He walked the length of the tree and spent time studying the roots, which seemed to convince him all was okay. He turned and called to the other man in the SUV.

The second man joined him and they got to work trying to clear the road. Isabelle watched intently, waiting for Adam or Nate to appear, but suddenly, out of the corner of her eye, she observed Claire stealthily climb from the vehicle with Laura in her arms. Ropes dangled from her wrists as she helped Mia out, clearly ready to make a run for it through the woods. Isabelle knew only too well the desperate fear that would make

Claire choose such a risky move. She had no way to know that her brother and his friend were there to save her.

Isabelle couldn't breathe. She clenched her hands against her thighs as she silently cheered them on. One step around the back of the SUV, two. One step more and they would be hidden.

Laura's wail pierced the silence.

The men dropped the tree and whirled around. As soon as they spotted Claire, they pulled weapons and shouted. Claire pushed Mia away. Isabelle watched her daughter cower behind the vehicle, and it was all she could do not to run to her, but wisdom dictated she stay hidden until Adam and Nate made their move.

Claire turned and ran down the road, obviously trying to pull the men's attention away from Mia. One man followed her. Nate darted out from hiding and jumped him, wrestling the mercenary to the ground as they struggled for control of the weapon.

Before Adam could grab the other man, he snatched Mia and ran into the woods—directly toward where she was hiding. Adam started to give chase, but a cry from Nate distracted him. The mercenary had broken loose and scrambled to his feet. He backed into the woods on the far side of the road, keeping his gun leveled at them until he reached the trees. He turned and dashed deeper into the forest.

"Go after Mia!" Nate shouted. "I'll track him."

As the mercenary dragged Mia through the trees, Isabelle could see the terror etched on her daughter's face. She had to do something to stop him from getting away with her little girl. Quickly, she scanned the ground for a branch or anything she could use as a weapon, yet found nothing she could swing without risking injury to Mia.

But she had another weapon. She didn't know how to use

it, but the kidnapper wouldn't know that, and she only had to hold him off until Adam caught up. Silently, she pulled the handgun from her pocket. She'd seen enough police dramas to know that she had to release the safety if she had a prayer of fooling him, so she located that part and rested her finger lightly on it, all while keeping an eye on the man advancing toward her. Mia was dragging her feet, which slowed him down and gave Isabelle time to step into position.

When they were just yards away, she breathed a prayer for confidence and stepped out in front of the man, assuming a spread-leg pose as she boldly raised the gun and pointed it at his head. "Stop right there."

The man laughed and whipped out his own gun. "Think again, lady. If you want to ever see your daughter alive, throw down the gun and let me go."

For a panicked moment, Isabelle wanted to kick herself. What had she been thinking to imagine she could take on a mercenary?

She hadn't been. She'd been a terrified mother watching a heavily armed man kidnapping her daughter. She tried to blank her mind, to think through how to get out of this stand-off and keep Mia safe.

Lord help me.

She had to keep him talking.

"If I toss down my gun, will you give me back my daughter?"

His harsh laugh in reply chilled her blood, reminding her this was a man without pity or scruples. He wouldn't hesitate to take out both of them.

She tightened her grip on the gun. Did she have the guts to try to shoot?

Out of the corner of her eye, she saw Adam stealthily approaching. She held her stance, keeping her eyes on the man while surreptitiously looking past him for a signal from Adam.

Adam made a motion with his hands that she read as *keep him talking.*

Isabelle avoided looking at her daughter, knowing that if she did she would come completely apart. "Why are you doing this? What do you want from us?"

"Look, lady, I'm not here for Sunday tea and chat. Put the gun down or I'll shoot you."

"Why?"

He looked exasperated. "So, you'll give us the baby."

Isabelle feigned confusion. "What are you talking about? I don't have the baby."

He shrugged. "My friend probably has her by now. You'd be wise to stop fighting."

Chills shivered through her at his evil tone. Adam had crept closer. Isabelle watched him holster his gun then reach down and come up with a rock. Now more than ever, she needed to distract the mercenary.

"And if your friend does have her?"

The man gave a harsh laugh that paralyzed Isabelle.

"Then you'd better hope that my boss is in a good mood."

Adam was so close now, Isabelle was terrified the man would hear him.

She let out a cry to cover him. "No! I can't depend on your boss. I don't even know him. Why would he want the baby?"

The man shot her a disgusted look. "To force her father to give us what we want. Now, put the gun down or—"

The rock coming down on his head halted whatever he had been about to say.

Isabelle dropped the handgun and charged forward, opening her arms to Mia and wrapping them tightly around her baby girl, just holding her close and absorbing her frightened sobs.

Adam glared at Isabelle. He was mad because she hadn't stayed at the car, and his feelings were justified, but she didn't want Mia to witness more anger. She angled her head to Mia and then shook it, hoping Adam would understand.

He nodded. "We'll talk later."

Adam cuffed and hogtied the mercenary. He didn't like leaving Isabelle alone with the man, but he was only semiconscious and posed no threat. "Can you stand guard over him while I find Nate, Claire and Laura? I'll come back for you."

Isabelle picked up on the thread in his voice that indicated he was not confident all was well back at the road. "Go ahead. I've got my brave girl to help me guard the prisoner."

"You have the keys to the patrol car? We need to retrieve it."

She handed them over and he loped off through the woods.

Once Adam was gone, Isabelle found a boulder to sit on. She brushed off the snow and gathered Mia onto her lap. "Oh, my baby girl." She kissed the top of her head. "That must have been so scary. You were so brave."

Mia looked up, her eyes wide. "You had a gun."

Isabelle spoke softly to reassure her. "Can I tell you a secret?"

Mia nodded.

"I have no idea how to shoot a gun. Mr. Adam gave it to me to scare off bad men so they would think I did." She hugged her daughter close. "But I promise, I would have figured out how to do it so I could keep you safe. Because that's my job—to protect you."

Mia snuggled into her arms, and Isabelle felt a huge sigh shudder through her body. She made a silent vow that when this was over, she was going to find the best child therapist money could buy to help her daughter cope with everything she had been through.

But that was later. Right now, she had to pray that Adam could rescue Laura, Claire and Nate.

Adam ran back through the woods in search of Nate, his thoughts racing as hard as his feet. Having to choose between chasing after Mia or helping Nate had torn him apart, but his training had made the choice clear. Nate stood more of a chance on his own than Mia did.

And then there was Isabelle. Adam had wanted to rage at her over her foolish actions, but in truth, he couldn't fault her. He should have known she was incapable of staying behind when all those she loved were in danger.

Did he fit into that category?

The errant thought caught him by surprise, and he brushed it quickly aside. Isabelle was grateful to him, but love didn't figure into their relationship. He was there to protect her and the children, nothing more, even if they did remind him of all that was missing from his life.

He broke through the edge of the forest onto the road. Nate was nowhere in sight and neither was Claire or Laura. Frustrated, he headed across the road to the silver SUV. A soft whimper caught his attention and he swiveled toward the forest on the far side of the road. A flash of blonde hair caught his eye.

"Claire," he called. "It's me."

His sister waved from behind a tree, but she didn't move to come forward. Fearing she was hurt, Adam dashed across the road. He found Claire huddled behind a tall pine, cradling Laura, who appeared uninjured.

"Where's Nate?"

Claire let out a shuddering breath. "He took off through the woods after the man. He told me to stay hidden here and not to come out for anything."

And his obedient sister had listened to Nate, unlike Isabelle, who had ignored his directions. But then, Claire wasn't a mother bent on protecting her child.

A crashing sound back in the woods alerted Adam and he stood guard, his back to Claire, blocking her from sight.

"Claire, it's just me." Nate ducked through some underbrush and emerged from the forest. He saw Adam and shook his head. "He got away. Had too much of a head start, and I didn't want to risk leaving Claire and Laura alone for too long with the other man at large."

"The other man is restrained."

At Nate's surprised look, Adam gave a chuckle. "Long story, but Isabelle is standing guard. Why don't you and Claire retrieve your car? I'll get Isabelle, Mia and our prisoner, and meet you back here. We'll have to deal with their vehicle, though."

Nate agreed. "I don't know who of my deputies I can trust at this point, so I'll call in the Bureau of Investigation to take custody of the SUV and our prisoners."

Adam tossed him the keys to the sheriff's car.

Nate helped Claire to her feet and steadied her. As they turned to walk up the road, he uttered a warning, "I don't have to tell you these guys mean deadly business. When we get back to Claire's, we need to find a safe house that no one knows about."

Nate's words echoed in Adam's mind as he made his way through the woods to Isabelle and Mia. Despite his concern to reach them, the forest began to work its magic. His heart rate slowed, his breathing became easier, and he had a sudden yearning to introduce Isabelle and Mia to the peace he felt. It was just the tonic they would need after these endless days of terror.

Suddenly he knew exactly where to take them, who to ask for help. His forest therapy guide was one person he knew he could trust. Matt was a clear example of how money didn't matter in the line of fire, but it sure made the recovery process more accessible. He had built several ski chalets in the mountains and routinely loaned them to fellow vets in need. Adam could easily borrow one, no questions asked.

And maybe, since they would be deep in the forest, he could teach Mia and Isabelle how to let nature heal them.

Adam breathed a sigh of relief as he arrived at the clearing and found Isabelle sitting guard, Mia asleep on her lap. His heart broke for all the trauma this child had experienced. She needed the forest, and he would give it to her.

SIXTEEN

Isabelle joined Adam beside an unmarked car and watched as a speck in the sky came close enough for him to point out his friend's private helicopter. They'd chosen the hospital helipad as the natural place to unobtrusively rendezvous.

A bark to their left drew attention away from the sky, and Adam turned just in time to see a bundle of gold fur streak across the parking lot and skid to a stop at his feet. He sank to his knees and burrowed his head in Chance's fur. "How'd you get here, buddy?"

Claire came running across the lot, out of breath. "We made it. I was afraid you'd be gone already."

Adam grinned at his sister and then turned to Mia, who'd come up beside him. "Not without Chance, right, Mia?"

"Right, Mr. Adam."

Adam hoisted her in his arms as the chopper descended. "Ready to go for a ride in the sky?"

Isabelle gazed at him in amazement. How could this man continually find the reserves to be so gentle with Mia when his wounds were repeatedly being triggered?

Adam hurried them across the tarmac as soon as the helicopter touched down. They were in their seats and off again within minutes. Claire stood on the ground, waving goodbye.

Isabelle hated leaving her behind in danger, but she'd refused to leave her dogs, and Nate had promised to keep her safe.

As the helicopter lifted into the sky, Isabelle sat back and breathed what felt like her first clear breath in a week. She wanted to close her eyes and sleep, but Mia had other ideas. Isabelle lifted her so they could sit, heads together, peering out the window at the mountains and marvel at the snowcapped peaks.

"Want to go sledding down those mountains?"

Mia giggled, but then her shoulders drooped.

"What is it, sweetie?"

"Aunt Jess promised to teach me to ski this winter."

Before Isabelle could summon a reply, Mia brightened. "Maybe Mr. Adam will."

The words brought a pang to Isabelle's heart. She couldn't bear to tell Mia that Adam would be out of their lives as soon as they were safe.

The sun was setting over the Rockies an hour later as Isabelle handed Mia down to Adam. She sucked in a deep breath of cold mountain air and sighed in pleasure. "This is extraordinary, Adam."

"Not my doing. Thank my pal, Matt."

Isabelle turned to the tall man she'd barely had a chance to meet as they'd loaded into the helicopter at the hospital. "I don't even know how to possibly thank you enough, sir."

"Matt. And no thanks necessary. Adam told me what you're doing for your friend. That's mighty brave."

Adam spoke up. "I've got a little girl here who seems in need of food. What do you think? Shall we go inside?"

Matt showed them into the house, a gorgeous A-frame nestled into the side of a mountain in the heart of the Rockies.

After a quick tour that included a fully stocked freezer and pantry, Matt took his leave. "I need to head out before anyone suspects where I am. I'll fly on to California to draw attention away from here, in case anyone tried to track us. Make this your home. And stay safe."

Isabelle smiled gratefully. "You've given us that chance."

Adam walked Matt out. "Thank you."

Matt brushed the thanks aside. "You all right to do this? We didn't talk about that part."

Adam responded softly. "I am because I have to be…for them. But this…" He gestured to the forest crowding the back of the house. "This gives me what I need to rejuvenate."

Matt nodded. "I thought it might. Take care now. Call if you need anything."

Adam watched his friend disappear into the night sky, and then took a moment to just stand and breathe in the peacefulness of their surroundings.

He was under no illusion that they were out of danger but, for tonight at least, he could relax his guard and find his balance. With one last glance as the sun sank in the west and the indigo sky began to fill with stars, he decided he'd bring Mia out here before bed.

First, he had to feed her. He headed into the living room. Isabelle has been exploring the house while he saw Matt off, and she greeted him with a genuine smile relaxing her face.

"This place is amazing."

Adam returned the smile. "I was about to see what I can rustle up for dinner. What do you think, Mia? Any chance Matt left us chicken nuggets?"

Once they'd eaten their fill of chicken nuggets and mac and cheese, Adam carried the plates to the dishwasher. When Isabelle followed, he asked quietly, "Would it be okay if I took Mia out to see the stars?"

The smile that lit her face at his suggestion kindled a fire in his heart.

"Sounds lovely. I'll settle Laura in while you do that."

He bundled Mia into her jacket and scarf, and took her hand. "I want to show you something special. Let's go see the stars."

"We have stars at home. Sometimes Mama and I look at them together."

"I often watch them at home too."

"Maybe sometimes we're looking at them at the same time," she chirped.

Adam's heart swelled with joy. "Well, tonight we will be for sure."

He led her outside onto the rooftop balcony and stopped short. He'd been expecting to surprise Mia, but he found himself stunned by the magnificence.

Mia's voice was hushed with awe as she spoke. "Mr. Adam, look at them!"

Adam crouched beside her. "Do you see those stars up there, the three together like a belt?"

"That's Orion the Hunter," Mia told him. "Mama showed me him in a book and then we found him in the sky. The red star has a funny name, like a bug."

"Betelgeuse," Adam confirmed.

"If you lift me up, I think I could touch them."

Adam laughed and raised her as high as he could.

Her face fell. "I can't reach them."

Hearing her disappointment, he lowered her into his arms. "That's the beauty of nature, Mia," he said softly. "We just feel it inside even if we can't touch it." He paused. "Can you feel it?"

Mia was quiet for a long moment, and he smiled as he watched her scrunch up her face. "You don't have to try so hard. Just breathe softly and let your heart open wide."

Mia lifted her face to the stars, and he could feel her body relax as she slowly breathed in and out. He could tell the moment she let go and just let the joy fill her body.

"I can feel it, Mr. Adam," she whispered. "I can feel it."

Moisture sprang to Adam's eyes as he soaked in the peace of holding this precious little girl under the glorious star-studded heaven. In this moment, in this place, it was easy to believe in a future that held goodness.

They stood for a few minutes in rapt silence until he felt Mia begin to shiver. "I think it's time to go in, Stargirl. Take one good long look to bring into your dreams."

When Mia had done so, he turned to the door, but he stopped when he saw Isabelle standing there, watching them, her own eyes shimmering.

He handed Mia over to her. "Good night, Stargirl."

The look Isabelle shot him was part gratitude and part simmering with something he couldn't even allow himself to recognize but didn't want to lose. "Join me in the library once they're settled?"

She nodded and slipped away.

Adam took another minute to look up to the heavens and whispered a prayer. *Lord, help me keep them safe.*

Isabelle stopped in the doorway to the living room. The fear that held her back had nothing to do with the dangerous mercenaries who pursued them and everything to do with the dangerous feelings Adam was igniting in her. She couldn't do this again, couldn't let someone in who had the power to break her.

But Adam had asked her to join him, and she owed him far too much to reject such a simple request.

He had his back to her, poking at the fire, but he turned as she entered, as if her presence called to him as strongly as he called to her heart.

"Come in. I thought you deserved some hot cocoa and a fire after all you dealt with today."

There he went, thinking of her again, when his day had been every bit as stressful. When had anyone ever put her first like this? She shook away the alluring thought. "Thank you. That sounds lovely."

They settled on chairs opposite each other before the fire and, for a few minutes, made small talk about the house, the beautiful location—anything but the danger that dogged them. After a time, Isabelle broached a topic that intrigued her.

"You seem so at home in the wilderness. Did you grow up here?"

He shook his head. "Nope, I was raised a city boy."

"Wow, I would never have guessed."

Adam dipped his head and hesitated so long that Isabelle feared she'd offended him.

"The wilderness, it saved me." He took a sip of his cocoa, then stood and walked to the plate-glass window that dominated the eastern wall.

"When I was medically discharged from the army, I was a mess—physically and mentally. The physical wounds healed, for the most part. I'll have symptoms from the brain injury for the rest of my life. You've seen some of them, like the headaches." He leaned forward in what looked like physical pain as he scrubbed his hands over his face.

When he raised his eyes to look at her, the agony in them ripped through her heart. She wanted to tell him to stop talking, to spare himself the pain of reliving it, but something told her he needed to share his story.

"The emotional wounds weren't as noticeable as the ones that left visible scars, but their pain was worse. When Nate invited me to visit him here…well, there's no easy way to say it. I was broken. I had nothing to lose."

He turned and stared into the night beyond the window.

"I found myself again out there. In the forest, the mountains. The quiet silenced all the noise in my head. I could just...be."

He shrugged away from the window and came back to sit across from her again. "Slowly, I began to heal. Not completely. I'll never be the man I was. But on good days, I like to think I'm someone better."

Isabelle leaned forward and reached out to touch his hand. "Obviously, I didn't know you before, but the man you are now...he's pretty special."

Adam closed his eyes and breathed in deeply. "Thank you."

She sighed. "I only wish..." The words drifted away. She didn't want to mar the evening with thoughts of Daniel.

"You wish what?"

She shrugged it off. "It's nothing."

"Isabelle," he said gently, "I bared my soul to you. What I told you, it's not something I talk about. But I wanted you to know that part of me. And I knew it was safe to tell you."

He took her hands in his. "I want you to have that safety, too, to know you can tell me anything."

She closed her eyes, and her hands fell away from his. Was that what they were doing? Exchanging pieces of their souls into each other's safekeeping? Somehow helping each other heal amid all the danger?

She raised her head and locked her gaze onto his. And the words began to pour out.

"The other morning, when you were making the pancakes, it..." She stumbled, unable to find the words.

"It triggered a memory," Adam supplied.

She nodded and looked away. "I've never told anyone, not even Jess. It felt... I guess it felt too private. But I want to tell you, so you'll...understand."

She lifted her mug, cradling it in her hands and stared blindly at the cocoa as she began. "I told you that Daniel also struggled with PTSD. But he was different than you. He wouldn't acknowledge that he needed help. His treatment came from a bottle." She paused, needing to stop the bitterness seeping into her voice.

"The morning of his last deployment, Daniel took Mia out for breakfast. It was supposed to have been father-daughter time, something they'd never had much of." She paused to take a sip of her cocoa because her mouth had gone suddenly dry at the memory.

"Based on eye-witness reports, Mia had been enjoying her favorite chocolate-chip pancakes while Adam's breakfast had been mostly liquid, poured from a flask into his coffee." Isabelle closed her eyes, remembering what had saved Mia's life. "Mia needed to use the restroom. She'd barely been potty-trained at the time. A kind waitress took her in. When they came back out, Daniel was gone."

Tremors shook her body and Adam stood and draped a blanket across her shoulders. He sat on the coffee table in front of her, took the mug from her hands and clasped them in his, giving her the strength to continue.

"The waitress called me to come get Mia." She gripped his hands hard. "I drove right by Daniel's wreck without even realizing it was his car. Apparently, he walked away and hitched a ride to the base. I was so furious with him after talking to the waitress that I barely spoke to him when he called to say goodbye. He tried to apologize, promised he would do better. I so badly wanted to believe him. It was only later, after he'd already left, that the garage called about the car." She shuddered. "The back, where Mia's car seat was attached, was so badly crushed, she never could have survived."

Tears poured down Isabelle's face, but she had to finish. "He deployed that afternoon and never returned."

She was trembling so badly by the time she finished that

Adam pulled her to her feet and into his arms. He wrapped them around her and held her close to his heart, gently stroking her hair and whispering soothing words. They stood like that for a long time, the fire crackling, the aroma of the burning wood edging past Adam's fresh scent and filling her senses. Isabelle wanted nothing more in that moment than to stay in his arms forever, to be able to open her heart to loving him, but the scars ran too deep.

She pulled back and reached a trembling hand up to cup his cheek. "Thank you. You are the best man I have ever known."

He raised his hand to cradle her head and, as he leaned forward, she knew he meant to kiss her. She allowed herself a moment to gaze deeply into his eyes, but then she pulled away.

"Good night, Adam. I hope your dreams are filled with stars."

SEVENTEEN

Adam couldn't sleep. The pain of Isabelle's story pierced his heart while thoughts of her in his arms tormented him. Isabelle, Mia, Laura, they represented all the love and the family he'd always longed for but couldn't have. Even though his arms ached with the memory of holding Isabelle, she'd been right to pull away before he'd made the foolish mistake of kissing her. He was still a broken man. He couldn't give her the healing she needed.

But he could protect her. He rose and went to the window. The sky was growing lighter, the stars that had promised such wonder dimmed by sunlight that teased on the eastern horizon, reminding him a new day and responsibilities lay ahead. Resolve tightened in his gut. He would do whatever it took to give Isabelle and the girls safety and a future free from fear. And then he would say his final goodbye.

The aroma of coffee alerted him to Isabelle's presence before he noticed her standing by the window. He indulged for a moment, just drinking in the beauty of the woman who'd captivated his heart.

She turned when she heard his footsteps and offered a tentative smile. "You couldn't sleep either?"

He shook his head, afraid what he would say if he dared to speak.

"Come, look. The sunrise is spectacular. It makes up for the loss of sleep."

He couldn't help himself. He walked slowly until he was standing beside her. Sunlight danced over the tops of the snow-laden pines in a spectacular show of glory.

"See the way the sun's rays shine down?" Isabelle murmured. "It's like God is extending His hand to the world saying, 'Look what I've given you.'" She tilted her head to look up at him. "That's how I survived, you know. I learned to trust in God."

Adam glanced back at her, at the way the rays lit her face and gilded her hair, and his heart echoed the words. *Look what God has given into your care.*

He turned away abruptly. "We need to start go—" The words died on his lips as he noted the papers strewn across the table.

"Going through Jess's stuff. Yes, I started." She shrugged. "It seemed better than staring at the ceiling."

Adam picked up the coffeepot and filled his mug. "Should I top off yours?"

"No, thanks. I made it for you. I'm still sticking with tea. Come, let me show you what I found. I have no idea what any of it means, but maybe you will."

Isabelle had spread out the contents of the knapsack, the rolls from the cylinder sitting beside it still tightly clipped. Adam removed the clip and started to unroll the papers. "These are blueprints."

"I guess that makes sense if Nate said Jess's husband was a military engineer. What are they for?"

"I don't know yet, but I'll hazard a guess it's what the guy in the woods was talking about when he said they wanted her to force Laura's father to give them what they want."

Isabelle resumed reading Jess's journal while Adam pored over the blueprints. He had no relevant training, but between the notes in the margin and the images that took shape before his eyes, he understood exactly why the mercenaries wanted Laura.

His gut clenched as he recalled his brief conversation with Matt on the helicopter ride. Matt had maintained close ties with the military, and as he'd related what he'd known, Adam's concerns for Jess, Isabelle, and the girls had grown exponentially.

According to Matt, Alexander William James III had been a highly decorated soldier who'd become too well known for his reckless ways and ruthless actions. Reliable in getting the job done but bad for army PR, he'd put diplomatic relations at risk. He'd been censured and, when that hadn't stopped him, he'd been court-martialed. He'd vanished before the trial, and no one had heard anything until rumors arose of a man they called Silver Wolf who commanded a band of mercenaries so ruthless even the cartels were afraid of them. At first, Silver Wolf had accepted only missions in support of the United States. He'd accepted assignments the military considered too risky and beyond the pale. Nothing had been officially sanctioned, but no one stopped him. Until things went south.

Matt had said it wasn't exactly clear what was truth and what had become myth, but Silver Wolf was believed to be James. He had severed ties with the US and now worked for the highest bidder. No one knew the exact size of his band of mercenaries, but they had a reputation as the wildest, most vicious outlaws on the planet.

Now they were after Laura. And only Adam and Isabelle stood in their way.

"Adam, what's wrong?"

Adam jerked his head up. "What?"

"I can read your body language. What did you find?"

"The reason James is so determined to get Laura." He swallowed hard. "These blueprints her father created are for brilliant designs that will enhance the mobility and reach of troops while elevating their security." He swallowed hard. "But in the wrong hands…"

He couldn't even allow himself to voice the thought, but he knew one thing for sure. James, Silver Wolf—regardless the name he was using— he needed to be stopped. Whatever it took.

The rest of the morning passed quickly as they studied the clues Jess had left. The girls, exhausted from days of adventure, slept soundly, and when they woke, Isabelle took a break to play with them. When he finished with the papers, Adam set himself to tinkering.

"What are you making?"

"I got these from Claire before we left. She uses them to track dogs that get away. I figured I'd make an anklet for you and each girl, so that in the event something happens, I'll be able to find you."

By noon, Adam had finished the trackers and made a playful ceremony of attaching one to each of the girls and Isabelle. "Special bracelets for the special ladies in my life. Now, who wants to have a snowball fight?"

Isabelle laughed. "Had enough of espionage for one morning?"

His expression sobered. "Sometimes you need to be reminded of what it's all for. Come on, Mia. You look like a champion snowball maker."

Mia's giggle warmed Isabelle's heart. Adam's attention was so good for her.

"Why don't you two play while Laura and I round up some lunch?"

"Sounds good. Come on, Mia. Let's go build us an appetite."

The music of Mia's squeals of joy peppered with Chance's

happy barks provided background as Isabelle cooked. With Laura strapped to her back, she chatted to the baby and kept anxious thoughts at bay.

Until the first streaks of flame soared past the kitchen window, quickly followed by at least ten more.

"Adam! Mia?" Isabelle dashed for the door into the yard. She flung it open and raced outside.

An arm swung out and wrapped itself around her neck. The roar of a helicopter swooping overhead, shooting flares around them, drowned her screams for help.

Isabelle wrestled with the man as he tried to unlatch Laura's carrier, but she was no match for his strength. He flung her aside and took off into the woods with Laura.

Isabelle stumbled to her feet and tried to give chase, but he was too far ahead. Her roar of pain echoed through the mountains.

Adam came running around the house. "What happened?"

"He took Laura." She pointed at the woods.

Adam picked up the baby blanket that had fallen to the ground. "Chance."

The dog was at his side in a moment. Adam held the blanket for him to sniff. "Seek Laura." The dog took off through the woods. "He's not really trained in scent detection, but Goldens are naturally good at air scents. Take Mia back inside. I'm going after Chance."

Isabelle took Mia and started in, but a whiff of smoke caught her attention. She ran to the corner of the house and screamed when she saw flames racing across the lawn. Intentional or not, the flares had set the mountain on fire!

Isabelle rushed inside to call for help. From the window, she could see the helicopter hovering, no doubt waiting for the man with Laura, but the winds from the rotors fanned the flames and the fire was rapidly growing out of control. She fell to her knees and raised her voice in prayer.

"Dear Lord, protect Adam and Chance and help them find Laura in time for us to get off this mountain."

EIGHTEEN

Isabelle glanced at her phone. It had been less than five minutes since Chance had torn into the woods after Laura, but already the flames had spread, licking along the underbrush and leaping from tree to tree on the perimeter of the property. The road was wrapped in smoke and visibility was decreasing by the minute.

Terror wound through her heart, but she tried to put up a brave front. "Mia, help me gather these things so we're ready when Adam comes back." Her lips whispering prayers, Isabelle repacked all of Jess's papers and their bags and brought them down to the garage where Matt had showed them the truck he kept for emergencies. She buckled Mia into the back, then grabbed some cloths from a stack and soaked them with water. "Keep this for your face."

With nothing left to do, she turned on the ignition and hit the remote for the garage door. Slowly the door rose, revealing an inferno. Panic took hold and, for a moment, she feared her eyes were deceiving her, but the wind shifted and she saw Chance emerge from the flaming woods with the baby carrier in his mouth, Adam racing behind him. Isabelle sank against the hood of the truck. *Praise the Lord.*

"Adam," she shrieked. "Over here."

Adam paused then veered off in her direction. When they

reached the truck, he took the baby and handed her over to Isabelle, all while lavishing praise on Chance. He grabbed a towel and soaked it with water to rub over his buddy. Chance bounded into the back seat, next to Mia. Adam closed them in while Isabelle climbed into the front, cradling Laura. He ran around the front of the truck, hopped in, and set off through the fire.

Isabelle had been frightened when the men had first chased her through the woods to Adam's house. She'd been frightened each time they'd been pursued on dangerous roadways, and she'd been terrified when she'd had to fight off a mercenary holding her daughter hostage, but none of those even approached the magnitude of terror that paralyzed her now.

Flames leapt through the cloud of dark smoke that obscured the road. Adam had the truck lights on, but they couldn't penetrate the density. Trees crackled and popped beside them, making the entire mountain feel apocalyptic. Sparks showered down upon them as flames danced across the roadway. She glanced at Adam. His expression was grim, but his hands were steady on the wheel. Had he driven through similar conditions while deployed? And then the follow-up thought—was this triggering him? Would he be able to maintain his focus?

She breathed in and said a prayer.

From the back seat, she could hear Mia. "Mr. Adam, how can the fire burn snow?"

Isabelle chuckled despite herself. "Good question. I have no idea."

"Mr. Adam, you know, right?"

Adam's grimace gave way to a smile. "As it happens, I do. Remember the fire we saw come from the helicopter? Those were flares that firefighters sometimes use to stop fires. They're strong enough to make the snow evaporate."

"But the bad men used them to start a fire instead?"

"They did."

"I think we need to pray for them."

Isabelle hadn't thought anything could make her feel better, but her small daughter's faith did. "Yes, Mia. Let's pray for them."

The acrid smoke was filtering through every miniscule opening in the truck as Adam eased along the burning road. Laura started to cry and Mia started to cough. Isabelle's throat was burning.

"Just a little longer," Adam promised mere seconds before a burning tree crashed down on the road before them.

Isabelle choked back a shout as Adam pressed the accelerator and drove the truck over it. In her mind, she was picturing flames licking along the bottom of the borrowed vehicle. *Please, God, save us.*

Ahead, the sky began to lighten. Sirens began to drown out the roar of the flames as they finally outraced the inferno that had blazed through the forest, consuming everything in its path.

Isabelle allowed herself to relax and drew in a breath. Immediately she started coughing and realized her mistake.

"Open the window," Adam directed. "The air down here is clear enough."

Firetrucks raced by them heading up the mountain, but Adam didn't stop until he reached the staging area in a campground.

He pulled in and was immediately surrounded by firefighters.

"What happened? Is there anyone else up there?"

"Not sure," Adam responded. "We were staying at a cabin near the summit that belongs to a friend, but I don't know if there are any other structures nearby."

"Who's your friend?"

Adam gave him Matt's full name and the fire chief nodded in recognition. "He owns the mountain and his is the only dwelling. We'll keep searching, but it's likely there's no one else."

"There were at least two other people," Adam countered. "The ones who started the fire. One was shooting flares from a helicopter. The other ran off through the woods." He lowered his voice. "They're mercenaries."

That single word triggered a round of questioning. Adam finished answering what he could and gave Nate's name as a reference. While he waited for the fire captain to speak with Nate, Isabelle had the emergency techs check the girls.

The captain returned, his demeanor solemn. "Your friend said to call him. Said it was urgent."

Adam glanced to where Isabelle was still speaking with the techs, thanked the captain, and stepped aside to make the call.

"Nate, what's up?"

"I have a suspicion how you're being tracked."

"I'm listening."

"The deputy who found Isabelle's phone. It was Warren. Check her phone. I'm thinking they loaded some sort of tracking into it, and then Warren pretended to find it in the bushes."

Frustration gnawed at Adam. Why hadn't he thought of that? But blame was useless. Isabelle's phone had been returned to her only a day into this bizarre escapade. Back when they'd had no clue how convoluted and deep this web ran.

"I'm taking her off-grid. We'll decoy the phone. I'll be in touch."

"Where do you mean off-grid?"

He hadn't noticed Isabelle come up behind him. He signaled for her to wait and then disconnected from Nate.

"Let's get in the truck and I'll explain."

"Adam…"

He hated the trepidation in Isabelle's voice, but this time it was justified. They'd been tracked everywhere they'd gone. But at least now he knew why.

Quickly he explained Nate's theory about the phone. "So, we need to dispose of it, and then disappear. I have a small cabin up in the mountains about an hour from home. No one knows about it. It's where I go when I need to be alone. We'll bring some supplies and hole up there while I finalize plans."

"What kind of plans?"

He glanced over at her. She wasn't going to like this either. "I spoke to Matt earlier. We're creating a group to take James down."

"You're mounting a mission."

"You could call it that, I guess."

"Against arguably the most dangerous mercenary on earth?" The ice in her voice stunned him. "I'm not following."

"You can't resist it can you? You just have to take on another mission. You need to take down the bad guys."

Adam blinked, sure he'd just misunderstood, but when he glanced at Isabelle, he knew he was wrong. Her expression had hardened, and she was taking no prisoners. Still, he had to try.

"Isabelle, we have to stop them. These are the men who are holding your friend and her husband, who've pursued us for days, tried to kill you, managed to kidnap Laura twice. They won't stop unless we stop them."

"But why you? You've already been through so much. You've already risked everything."

He was quiet. There was no answer that could make her understand. This was so much bigger than them; so much more was at stake. From the moment he'd seen those drawings and known the type of work Jess's husband was capable of, he'd realized there was no turning back. If James and his men weren't stopped, no soldier would be safe from the destructive power of these mercenaries.

He wished Isabelle could understand that. But whether she could or not, his decision was made.

He looked over at her. Her eyes were closed. Whether she was actually asleep, or feigning it, the conversation was clearly done...as was any chance of them ever building a life together. A part of his heart broke for the death of what might have been. He glanced in the rearview mirror at Laura and Mia sleeping soundly. From the start, he'd insisted he wasn't interested in a relationship, but this brave little family had crept into his heart and laid claim without him even trying to mount a defense. Broken as he was, he'd allowed himself to hope.

And now that hope was crushed. If Isabelle couldn't understand why he needed to do this—not just for her, but for all the women and men he'd served with, for all those serving now and in the future, for men like her husband who had been broken beyond healing—then she really didn't understand him at all. There really was no chance for them. And that realization destroyed him more completely than any enemy weapon ever could have.

NINETEEN

The mountain retreat was lovely, yet Isabelle found neither peace nor joy in it. She and Adam were now on opposite sides of a battle she didn't even understand.

On the surface, nothing had changed. He played with Mia and took the girls for walks in the woods. She never joined them. It was too painful to see him in his element, to miss the new life she'd started to yearn for.

She was standing at the kitchen window watching Adam and Mia try to build a snowman when the first vehicle rolled up. Her heart kicked into instinctive panic until she saw Adam abandon the snowman to go welcome his friend. Isabelle recognized Matt the minute he stepped from the truck. What was he doing here?

Over the next hour, several more vehicles arrived, each carrying men and women in outdoor gear similar to the camouflage Adam had worn that second day they'd trekked through the woods. Dreadful certainty settled in her gut. He was gathering a team for his mission.

She kept her distance, not willing to interfere but terrified of being drawn in. When Adam had first said they were coming to the mountains, she'd hoped for a reprieve. That finally they had escaped the mercenaries long enough to catch their breaths, maybe even to explore the feelings that had surfaced between them.

But that was all gone now, lost in a combat mentality she knew all too well.

Mia was tired from her morning in the snow, so Isabelle settled in bed with her to read a story. By the end of the third page, her little girl's eyelids were drooping and by the end of the story, she was sleeping sweetly.

Laura was cranky and in need of a bottle, so Isabelle eased away and headed to the kitchen. She stood at the same window where she'd earlier watched Adam and Mia play, but now she saw Adam alone. He was leaning against a tree, just at the edge of the forest. He was looking away, but she could see his tortured profile and knew he was in the grips of an attack.

She wanted to run to him, to comfort him, but a part of her wanted to yell, *See what you're doing to yourself?*

The thought stopped her cold. No. He hadn't done this, at least not from the start. Shivers ran through her body as guilt washed over her. She'd done this to him. She'd brought this upon him when she'd pounded on his gate demanding he save her.

Blindly, she picked up Laura and the bottle. She needed some place private to grapple with these revelations. When she reached the end of the hall, she stopped to catch her breath and decide where to go. This house was unfamiliar and over-flowing with men and women in various versions of para-military dress. She needed a place away from the noise and the distraction.

Mia was asleep in her bedroom, so she couldn't go there. Mentally, Isabelle reviewed the layout of the house. There was a closed-in porch overlooking the river. Maybe she could find privacy there.

The porch was quiet, which only amplified the thoughts

racing around her brain. Laura started to cry and Isabelle tried to soothe her, but she wanted to cry, too. All the stress of the past days was getting to her, all the attempts to kidnap Laura, all the near-death experiences, the constant danger to her children, the growing attraction to Adam. And the broken heart that was sure to result.

It would be easy to write off her attraction as hero worship for the man who'd protected her, but she knew that it was Adam's wounded soul, his kind heart, that called to her. She'd fallen for the tinkerer, not the soldier—not that she didn't appreciate the warrior who protected children. But it was his soft side, the way he talked with Mia... She sniffled, thinking of him showing Mia the stars. Her thoughts were interrupted by the door opening.

A man in fatigues stepped out onto the porch, closing the door behind him. When he saw Isabelle, he stopped short. "Oh, sorry. I didn't realize you were out here."

"We were looking for some privacy," Isabelle answered.

Ignoring her comment, he strode toward them. "Hello, sweetie." He reached out a hand to touch Laura, and Isabelle jerked her away. Laura started to cry again.

He reached for her. "I'm good with babies. I can calm her."

Isabelle didn't want to be rude to one of Adam's buddies, but the man was getting on her nerves. "She'll be fine if you just leave us in peace."

The man walked to the door and flipped the lock.

Panic ratcheted through Isabelle. This *was* one of Adam's friends, wasn't it? Or had one of the mercenaries just blended in?

"Why did you lock the door?"

The man tilted his head and smirked. "Smart lady like you must have already figured out the answer to that." He extended his arms. "I'll take the baby now."

Isabelle backed toward the porch door that opened by the river. "I don't think so."

If she screamed, would Adam even hear her? She opened her mouth to try, but she'd barely gotten a squeak out before the man had his arm around her neck and a gun pressed to her side. "Give me the baby."

Isabelle tightened her arms around Laura. With everything she had learned about his boss, there was no way she could turn Laura over to this mercenary. As she shifted Laura, her hand brushed the bracelet Adam had made as a tracking device. Suddenly, she knew what to do. "You'll have to take me too."

He shrugged. "No problem. Two for the price of one." He whipped a rag from his pocket and gagged her. "You give me any trouble at all, and I take the baby and leave your body behind, got it?"

Isabelle nodded. The terrifying thought occurred to her that the only reason he wasn't shooting her now was that someone would hear. She had to cooperate or he'd make good on his threat. She just had to buy some time until Adam realized they were gone.

But after the harsh words she'd spewed at him, she didn't expect he'd be looking for her anytime soon. Maybe when Mia woke…

Her heart broke thinking of her sweet Mia. She prayed as the man dragged her off the porch and onto the waiting boat.

Oh, Dear Lord, please protect us all.

Adam was trying to concentrate on the conversation and the plans they were discussing, but his thoughts kept turning to Isabelle, rehashing every detail, and wondering how things could have gone south so fast.

Matt nudged him. "You okay, man?"

Adam nodded, but he knew he wasn't. That didn't matter now. He had to lock down his heart and focus on the mission.

They'd been working on their plan for over an hour when a sleepy-eyed Mia wandered into the room. "Mr. Adam, do you know where my mama is?"

Adam glanced up then signaled to Matt to take over. He lifted Mia into his arms. "Let's go find her."

Five minutes of searching turned into ten, and he found no trace of Isabelle. Concern gave way to fear, but he couldn't let on to Mia. "Maybe your mama took Laura for a walk. Let's get you a snack, and I'll go look for her outside."

He signaled to one of the women, figuring Mia would be more comfortable with her. "Can you take Mia to the kitchen for a snack? I have to find Isabelle. Stay there and we'll come back."

Panic was threatening Adam with each passing moment, but he had to get it under control. Chance suddenly head-butted him, and Adam breathed a sigh of relief. He knelt and wrapped his arms around his friend's neck and buried his face in his scruff. His heart rate began to settle and his thoughts to clear.

The tracking devices.

He took one last moment of peace from Chance and jumped to grab his phone from his pocket. He flipped open the tracking app and waited for the satellite to retrieve the signal. Mere seconds that felt endless. The results sent him back to his knees. Both Laura and Isabelle's devices were tracking deep in the mountains. His best estimate, they were an hour away.

All the time he'd been fuming and then plotting a mission, Isabelle and Laura had been in the grip of a mercenary bent on vengeance.

Guilt swamped him. Isabelle was right. He was no better than her husband. He'd neglected his primary duty of keeping them safe in favor of an ambitious paramilitary plan. And now she and Laura were paying the price.

How had this happened?

The only possibility was that somebody had gained access. One of his buddies? Was it possible one of them had really switched allegiance?

Suddenly, Adam didn't know who to trust. Any one of the men here could be in cahoots with the mercenaries. Panic clutched his throat, spots danced before his eyes, his heart was racing hard enough that he could feel it pounding in his throat.

Chance nudged his leg, but the panic attack was too intense. He needed something stronger than his fear. He needed—

God.

Isabelle's words from the sunrise conversation came back to him. *I learned to trust in God.* Adam breathed in the memory and prayed. Slowly, his heart rate settled, his brain cleared, and he began to plan.

He would have to trust Matt because he needed a helicopter. That was the only chance they had of getting to her in time.

In time for what? His brain shut out the question. His focus had to be only on what was productive.

He uttered a prayer that he was making the right decision. He'd briefly wondered if Matt had betrayed them when they'd been located on the mountain, but Nate's discovery of the tracking on Isabelle's phone let him dismiss that thought. He would have to check with Matt and then trust his instincts.

Adam took out his phone and sent a message asking Matt to join him on the porch. It was the only place he could think of where they could talk with complete privacy.

As he opened the door to the porch, he knew instantly that this was where Isabelle and Laura had been taken from. There was no sign of any scuffle, but the back door was open and banging in the wind.

"Adam?"

Adam waved him over and Matt stepped out on the porch.

"What's going on?"

"Shut the door."

Matt pushed it shut and strode across the porch to where Adam waited by the door.

"Isabelle and the baby have been taken. I'm pretty sure this is where they went out."

"Are you sure? Maybe the wind just blew the door."

Adam held up his phone with the tracking app open. "After the attacks on the road, I created an anklet for each of them that tracks their location. You can see where Isabelle is."

Matt whistled. "That's out near Mesa Verde."

"Can you get us in there?"

Matt took out his phone to check his weather app. "Dicey, but if we go soon, we'll make it. Winds are picking up, though."

"You know these men better than I do. Who can I trust to take care of Mia?"

"After this, I won't vouch for anyone. What if we swing by home, drop her with Claire, and pick up Nate? Three of us will be better."

Adam agreed. "But don't tell anyone we're leaving. I'll get Mia and meet you at the truck. Let's take yours. Mine is blocked in."

"Okay, but before we go, I know you had to decide to trust me." He held Adam's stare. "You can."

Adam forced himself to walk toward the kitchen, but his mind was already racing ahead to the car. He grabbed Mia's coat from the rack and picked up Chance's leash. He fixed a smile to his face and walked into the kitchen. "Hey, Mia, let's go take Chance for a walk."

"Where's Mama?"

"She's with Laura."

He could sense the barrage of questions to come, so he signaled Chance, who started to nudge at Mia.

"I think he needs to go out fast." She giggled.

Within ten minutes, they were in the truck headed to the field where Matt had landed his helicopter. The winds buffeting the vehicle amped up his nerves, but Adam focused on trusting God.

Mia had been very quiet on the whole ride, but as he lifted her into the helo, she touched his chin to get his attention. "The bad men have Mama, don't they?"

"We'll get her back, I promise." Adam was aware he'd never made a more serious vow in his life.

"I know you will, Mr. Adam."

"What's that prayer you prayed with your mama? Remember, in the car?" It felt like a lifetime ago that icy streets had been the worst of their problems.

"Jesus, I trust in You."

"Jesus, I trust in You." Adam held Mia's hand and repeated the prayer over and over as the helicopter fought the winds and finally lifted in the air.

TWENTY

They'd been driving for hours. Isabelle was exhausted, and Laura was fretting, so she reached for a bottle. Earlier, she'd demanded they stop for supplies. The mercenary had chosen an out-of-the-way store, and he'd held Laura, thus ensuring Isabelle's cooperation. But at least the baby had nourishment.

"How much farther?"

"What's it to you?"

"I'm just wondering how you were planning to drive all this distance alone with a baby? Do you even know how to care for her?" She was irritating him with her questions, but she needed to stay defiant or she'd give in to despair.

Satisfied after her bottle, Laura nestled into Isabelle's arms and fell back asleep. Isabelle fiddled with the anklet, wishing she could use it to send Adam some sort of message. She had no doubt that given more time he could have come up with something like that. He was so clever.

But he probably wasn't interested in what she thought of him.

Even if he did manage to rescue them, he'd never forgive her for her words. What she'd done was unforgivable. She'd taken his weakness and used it against him. She was ashamed of herself. She'd give anything to make it up to him.

But in a way, maybe she could. If she could be brave, and

keep the trackers hidden, she could lead Adam right to his prey. Because he was right, such evil couldn't be ignored.

At some point she must have fallen asleep, lulled by the motion of the car and complete exhaustion. She woke as they were pulling into a compound. It was snowing, and she had no idea where they were.

Her heart sank as a gate closed behind them with a definitive clink. The car proceeded into the center of a courtyard where a garage door opened and they were suddenly inside a building. Her captor came around, opened the door, and forced her out. Armed guards stood beside the doorway. One of them phoned for authorization, and then she and Laura were quickly escorted down a long, sterile hallway into a room where they were abandoned.

Isabelle had tried to keep track of the path they'd followed, hoping against hope she would find a way back out. Now that they'd been left alone, she took the time to scope the room, looking to find something that would help them get free. Best to be prepared even though it was unlikely she'd get a chance. She knew better than to try to escape on her own. They didn't want her. Laura was their bargaining chip. They'd likely just shoot Isabelle on sight if she tried to escape.

Time crawled. Isabelle was beginning to wonder if anyone would ever come for them, or if just holding Laura captive was sufficient to their goal, when suddenly the room lit up as a wall of monitors came to life.

Isabelle nestled Laura against her chest to protect her from the sudden glare and stared at the screens, waiting to see their purpose.

The first one flickered to life and Isabelle gasped as Jess's image appeared on the monitor. She looked strained and exhausted, but she was alive.

"Jess!" Isabelle knew she shouldn't sound so jubilant. Certainly nothing in her friend's face indicated reciprocal joy. Understandable, given the circumstances and that her presence meant Laura had been captured.

The expression on Jess's face shifted and Isabelle realized a second screen had come into focus. The man whose face appeared was gaunt with marks that looked like burns. His body, though shrunken, seemed defiant at the same time, his eyes hollow, vacant—until they rested on the small child Isabelle held. There was a brief flicker of interest before they went blank again. Isabelle remembered in that moment that he had never seen his daughter before.

"Well, what do you think, Robert? Isn't she a little sweetheart?" The words were innocent, but the tone of the man's voice coming through the speakers was chilling.

"Wouldn't it be a shame if anything were to happen to her?"

Isabelle suppressed an instinctive shudder, knowing the man was probably watching for a reaction. His voice was different from that of the man who had brought her here, and she wondered if perhaps this was Silver Wolf himself.

She looked to the screens to see if his words had had any effect on Jess or her husband. If they had, it was imperceptible.

"Hold the baby up to the screen so Daddy can see her sweet face."

Isabelle looked at Jess and her husband, both still with eyes cast down. She decided to take her lead from them and ignored his instructions.

He was not pleased.

Isabelle's eyes scanned the room trying to locate the camera he must be using to observe her. There was one directly above the monitors, which would make sense if he wanted the baby to be directly in their line of sight.

Laura was fussing, so Isabelle seized the chance to stroll

around the room to try to console her. She walked to the front wall and stood beneath the monitors.

"Get back where we can see you."

Isabelle ignored him and continued to look for something she could use in defense. There was a poker by the fireplace, but he would be able to see if she picked that up. There was one way around that.

Quietly, she set Laura down on the ground. She knew she wouldn't have much time, so she inched her way toward the camera. It was too high to reach, so she pulled over a chair and climbed up. Leaning forward, she wrapped both hands around the camera and twisted. The camera came off in her hands.

She had no illusion that she was safe for long, and there was no place to hide, so she quickly scooped up Laura and hid her in the corner. "Jess, if you can hear me, tell me where you are."

Isabelle listened carefully to her friend's response as she grabbed a cushion from a chair and wrapped it in Laura's blanket as a decoy. Then she went to wait by the fireplace. She picked up the shovel and poked at the coals in the grate. When she found the hottest ones, she scooped them into the ash bucket and set it just behind her. She put the poker in the bucket, left it sitting in the coals, and stood facing the fire and rocking her pretend baby.

Within minutes, the door burst open and a tall silver-haired man entered. "Come here."

His voice was harsh, and Isabelle's instinct would have been to obey. Instead, she stared at him defiantly. "The baby is cold. I'm staying by the fire with her. If you want to talk to me, you come over here." Isabelle's heart was thumping so hard in her chest she was surprised he couldn't hear it, but she maintained an outwardly calm demeanor. She glanced surreptitiously at the monitors and could tell that Jess and her husband were listening closely even if they could no longer see.

Isabelle faced the man as he stalked toward her. "What do you want with us anyway?"

He snarled and gave an evil grin. Tilting his head at the screen, he taunted, "Why don't you ask them?"

Isabelle's body quaked, but she stood her ground. "Because I asked you."

"You think you're so smart, so bold." He advanced on her and she wrapped her arms tightly around the baby.

He was towering over her when Laura whimpered. His head swung around at the sound, but then he lunged at Isabelle. As he reached for the baby, Isabelle collapsed in a heap. He reached down, but she grabbed the poker and swung it around at his head. That set him back with an angry roar, but she knew it wouldn't stop him for long. Dropping her fake bundle, she grabbed the pail of hot coals and flung it in his face.

His bellow of pain would have given her remorse had he not been intent on such evil. Without sparing him more than a glance to make sure he wasn't following, she ran for Laura and dashed out of the room. She slammed the door closed behind her, hoping it would lock automatically, and took off down the hall, praying she could find a doorway.

Adam had hoped with the chopper they'd be able to cut off the car with Isabelle and Laura before they reached their destination, but the detour to exchange Mia for Nate had delayed them. He'd been watching the tracking device like a hawk. It hadn't moved in the last ten minutes, so either they'd stopped for some reason, or they'd arrived. Given the remote location, he suspected the latter.

Matt was using all his military training to keep the chopper flying just above the tree line, but the snow that had begun as light flurries was getting steadily stronger.

The three of them were talking on headsets, debating their best strategies and trying to create a rescue plan based on limited knowledge. Nate was in contact with local law enforcement, Matt concentrated on keeping them in the air, and Adam focused on tracking Isabelle and Laura.

"Looks like they've arrived," Adam said into his mic. "There's been no noticeable movement from the tracker in the past ten minutes. I'm looking at satellite imaging for the area and there appears to be a sizeable bunker-like structure in an open space."

"How far out are we?" Matt's voice came through the headset. "The snow is making visibility difficult, but it will also camouflage us. As long as it doesn't get too bad, I can use my instruments to land."

"They're on the move but inside the compound. Moving fast."

"Adam," Nate called. "We've got something at ten o'clock."

Adam peered out the left side of the helicopter and a mix of terror and elation lit through his veins. "That's Isabelle. Can you land, Matt?"

"Not this close. The rotor wash would blow her away. Get ready to rappel. I'll circle around and go low enough for you to descend, then I'll land in that clearing ahead."

As Matt swung the helicopter, Nate called out a warning. "Company coming around at six." He picked up the rifle Matt had shown them earlier. "I'll hold them off while you jump."

Adam didn't take his eyes off Isabelle as he quickly donned his gear. He shed his headset, replacing it with a helmet and radio, and waited for Nate to give him the signal. Once they were in position, he opened the door and began his rapid descent into a copse of trees.

Above his head, Nate was on sniper duty, and Adam watched as the lead mercenary fell. Two dropped back and ran inside, but the others kept going. Adam ignored them. Nate was a first-rate sharpshooter, and he had to trust that. His job was to rescue Isabelle and get her out of range.

The instant his boots hit the ground, Adam disengaged his harness and took off at a run. Isabelle stared at him in blatant disbelief as he emerged from the treeline. Without stopping to talk, he wrapped his arms around her and pulled her back beneath the trees. He suspected the two mercenaries had gone inside to retrieve antiaircraft weapons, so he knew they were running out of time.

"Can you run faster?" he shouted, trying to be heard over the roar of the rotors.

Isabelle didn't waste a breath on words but increased her pace. Adam took her deeper into the stand of trees, hoping that they would be less of a target. They stumbled over the uneven, snow-covered ground and paused for breath once they were behind the trees.

"Are you okay?"

Isabelle nodded.

"Laura?" He pointed to the wrapped shape in her arms.

Again, she nodded, gasping for breath.

"Matt is going to set the helo down as soon as we're in the clearing. Nate has reinforcements coming. I'll take Laura so we can run faster."

His heart eased at how quickly she handed over the baby, but when he tried to run, she tugged him back. "Jess and her husband are in that building."

Adam's heart sank.

He took her hand in his. "Let me get you to the helo, and I'll go back." He could see she wanted to protest, but he pulled her with him as he zigzagged his way through the forest, constantly aware of the gun-fighting behind and above them. As they neared the clearing, Adam glanced skyward.

Matt was circling the helicopter to set it down when Adam heard the distinctive pop of an RPG. He held his breath watching the rocket stream toward his friends, terrified he was about to see them be blasted from the sky.

Isabelle gripped his arm, and he stood frozen, listening for the explosion, mentally counting down Five…four…three…two… Then the tense moment, knowing the grenade would self-destruct in one. When the rocket exploded and the smoke cleared, Matt was ascending, having veered slightly to the left to avoid direct impact. But one of the rotors had been hit and the ship was wobbling.

Praise the Lord. Adam breathed a prayer of thanks that it hadn't been worse. Matt would be able to land safely, but it meant Adam and Isabelle were on their own until help arrived.

He motioned to Isabelle. "Back into the trees." They had no time to waste. He hated to even attempt this with a woman and child, but they would be sitting ducks if they stayed out there. Their best chance of surviving was to sneak into the building and find Jess and her husband while the mercenaries were busy trying to shoot down a helicopter that was now out of range.

They crept back, careful to stay hidden within the trees. When they were almost to the edge of the forest, he stopped. "What can you tell me about the layout?"

Isabelle closed her eyes and described it as best as she could from memory.

"Any sense of security? Guards, cameras?" It was a lot to ask of her, but he needed whatever she could recall.

She quickly recounted the details of her escape, and Adam's eyes grew wide with admiration. He was torn between leaving her hidden while he scoped out the building or taking her with him. It was an inestimable risk. Better he know where she was. He grabbed her hand and ran for the door.

Once they were inside, he stopped to take stock. The hallways seemed deserted, but there was a lot of foot traffic overhead, as if the mercenaries realized the compound was under attack.

"Do you have any idea where they're holding Jess?" he whispered to Isabelle.

"No. I asked before James appeared. She didn't know exactly, but she said she could hear a lot of running water."

"That's good. It sounds like she's on this level, hearing all the water draining through the house. We need to find the main drainpipe."

Adam searched the hall as far as he could see and found nothing, but the minute they rounded the corner, he knew they were in the right place. He could see the heavy pipe protruding from the ceiling and running into a wall between two doors. He cautiously approached the door, surprised there wasn't more security. He tried the handle. Locked.

"Is anyone in there?" he called.

A muffled response prompted Adam to force the lock. The pop was gratifying, and they cautiously entered to find Jess tied to a chair with a gag in her mouth. Adam removed the gag, then made quick work of the zip ties while he talked. "Do you know where your husband is?"

She nodded. "After Isabelle clocked James, he ran for help, forgetting that we were still on screen. We figured out Robert is just down the hall."

Noise overhead alerted Adam to incoming support just as Matt's voice came over his radio. "Backup has arrived and is engaging above."

"Tell them we're inside. I found Jess, and her husband is also here," Adam called into his radio. The last thing he needed was their allies bombing the building.

Within minutes, they'd located Robert, but evacuating him

proved more difficult. Months of captivity had taken their toll. He was emaciated and weak, barely able to stand on his own. Jess ran to him, but Adam maintained focus.

"Matt, any update?"

"Bunker is ninety percent secured. James is on the run in the building. Recommend sheltering in place."

"Roger that. Radio when clear."

Adam had begun to barricade the doors when Matt's urgent voice came over the radio. "Bunker is rigged to blow. James is about to detonate. Get out now."

TWENTY-ONE

"Isabelle, I'm going to put Robert in a fireman's hold. I need you and Jess to follow right behind until we get to the door. Once we get there, if all is clear, fan out and run to the woods."

The fear on her face could have paralyzed him.

"I need to know. Where's Mia?"

"Safe with Claire."

Her whole body relaxed with the news and Adam knew he could count on her.

He slipped his arm around Robert and lifted him onto his back just as explosions began to roll through the building.

"Scratch the plan. Run!"

The women took off ahead of him. Adam could feel the vibrations as the bombs detonated in a chain. The entire ground was rumbling, and memories of far too many similar situations in battle reverberated through his head. Not now. He couldn't give in now. They were so close.

"Adam, do it for Mia!"

He looked through his darkening vision to see Isabelle standing in the doorway, waiting for him. Her face was frozen in terror, but her eyes were defiant, calling to him, pulling him through.

As the floor pitched and split apart, he dashed the final few feet, grabbed her hand, and burst through into daylight.

Snow swirled around his head, delicate flakes dusted his shoulders, and he lifted his face to breathe in the crisp, clean air.

"We're safe. You did it. You saved them."

Isabelle's jubilant voice danced through his head.

He took her hand and pulled her into an awkward embrace. "No, we did it together."

The next hours passed in a blur as military personnel arrived to assume command. Jess, Robert and Laura were taken away for evaluation. Isabelle borrowed Adam's phone and called Mia, who told her she hadn't been worried because she knew Mr. Adam would find her.

Isabelle disconnected the call and sank against a tree. Night had fallen and stars were filling the sky now that the smoke and storm had cleared. She was reminded of that peaceful night on the mountain when she'd listened to Adam telling Mia to open herself to joy.

When had she forgotten how to do that? When had she gotten herself so tied in knots that she'd disconnected from the person she'd always been? She missed that carefree, joyous woman.

"Isabelle?"

As if her thoughts had summoned him, Adam appeared before her. "They're going to give us a ride into town. Matt's copter is damaged. We have a choice, stay in town or make the long drive home."

Ravaged was the only word Isabelle could think of to describe how Adam looked right now. Her tall, handsome hero looked absolutely ravaged. There was no way she could ask him to drive home. She summoned a smile. "Town sounds good."

They settled into a cute inn for the night. Adam saw her to her room. As he said good-night and started to leave, Isabelle called him back.

"I owe you an apology."

He smiled at her sadly and shook his head. "You owe me nothing."

She grasped his hand. "You're wrong. I owe you everything. But mostly I owe you an apology. Is there somewhere we could talk?"

He seemed to hesitate for a moment. "There's a back deck, but it's cold."

She shivered just thinking of the temperature, but she knew how much being outside revived him. "I'll bring a blanket and meet you out there."

When she walked out onto the deck, she saw that Adam had the fire pit burning and he'd pulled chairs close. She angled hers to face him.

"I'm so sorry for what I said to you…"

Adam made to brush it off, but she persisted. "I was wrong, in so many ways. You're nothing like Daniel. I've known that since we first met. But when you told me about the mission, I reacted as if you were him. I didn't understand why right away, but I've had time to think." She hung her head. "I lashed out at you because I felt guilty."

"Guilty? What did you have to feel guilty for?"

Isabelle fidgeted. "I brought all this upon you. You had treatment. You were recovering, and I dragged you right back into a battle for our lives. It wasn't fair of me to blame you for doing what needed to be done."

He started to interrupt, but she raised her hand and asked him to let her finish.

"This isn't about you or about your brain injury or your PTSD. It's about me, my failings. I couldn't save my own husband from himself. I failed Daniel, and I failed my daughter by losing myself in my own grief and guilt. I promised myself I would never do that to Mia again. But, instead, I did it to you. I failed you. I said awful, unforgivable things, deliberately giving you the wrong impression because I was scared. Scared to love again. Scared to risk a broken heart. Because when you told me you were going after Silver Wolf, I was afraid of losing you too. I'd brought this to your door, and I couldn't save you from it."

Adam buried his face in his hands and, for a long moment, she feared she'd gone too far.

Finally, he lifted his head, and his expression was grave.

"You are so wrong, Isabelle. You are the strongest woman I've ever met. You have to know, deep in your heart, that you did not fail Daniel. War failed him. The repeated injuries destroyed him."

"But I didn't make him get help."

Adam shook his head sadly. "Daniel is far from the only soldier who couldn't seek help. That's part of what is so complicated about this. Soldiers are groomed to be strong, self-reliant, to never admit weakness. It's a mindset, and a broken brain sometimes can't see its way around that in order to seek help.

"Please don't destroy your life out of some misplaced sense of blame. What you've done these past few days, the way you fought to protect these children, that showed courage worthy of the finest soldiers I've ever fought beside."

Tears stung her eyes as she tried to process his words. "But I still failed you. I set you back. I know because I've watched you. I've seen the toll this has taken on you."

Adam rose and walked to the edge of the balcony. He stood for a long moment staring up at the sky before he turned, took a deep breath, and spoke.

"You didn't fail me, Isabelle. You saved me. Before you pounded on my gates, I was a recluse afraid to step into the world for fear I'd panic. The only place I ever felt safe was in nature. But you, and Mia, and my football baby opened my heart again. You showed me that life could be more than safe. It could be good. You took a man who was broken and helped him begin to heal—just by being you."

He came and knelt before her. "I know I'm not cured. There will be days, hours, when I struggle, but I can promise you this, Isabelle. I will never give up fighting it. I will never let it ruin your life or Mia's life. I want to be a whole man, to be the love you deserve, the father Mia needs. If I thought I couldn't be, if I thought I couldn't promise to love and cherish both of you, I would walk away from you right now, because I love you too much to hurt you."

He sighed and sat back on his heels. "I'll confess, I was not going to say this. I was going to be noble and walk away, let you and Mia have a good life without the burden of a broken soldier to hold you back."

She opened her mouth to protest, but he stopped her.

"I'm not walking away. I'm only saying that because I want you to understand that if I thought that was what was best for you and Mia, I would disappear from your lives in a heartbeat."

A chasm opened in Isabelle's heart. The idea of being without this man in her life was devastating.

Adam wasn't done. "A chaplain shared this quote from Isaiah at a very low point in my life. *But they that wait upon the Lord shall renew their strength; they shall mount up with wings as eagles; they shall run, and not be weary; and they shall walk, and not faint.*"

He leaned in and grasped her hands in his. "You say you brought danger to my door, but in my heart, I know it was God bringing you. Because we are meant to heal together, to build a life." He paused, then continued, his voice cracking, "Please say you'll give us that chance."

Isabelle closed her eyes, absorbed his words, and then pulled their clasped hands to her heart. Opening her eyes, she stared into his. "I love you, Adam. I love you so much. And if you'll have me, then yes. Yes, I absolutely accept that chance for a life with you."

EPILOGUE

Four months later

Adam and Isabelle emerged from the forest, arms wrapped around each other, faces wreathed in smiles. They'd left Mia and Chance at home with Claire so they could have time alone together in their favorite place to celebrate their recent engagement.

Now, as they approached the house, another smile lit Isabelle's face when she recognized the car in the driveway. "Jess is here?" Isabelle paused to correct herself. "I know, she's really Julia, but that's going to take some getting used to. Did you know they were coming? Is Robert out of the hospital?"

Adam just grinned, so Isabelle pulled away and rushed inside.

In the living room, she found her friend cuddling Laura, while a vastly improved Robert sat with his arm around them both. Isabelle stopped short as tears welled. She beamed at Adam, who had come up beside her. "You made this possible," she whispered.

Before he could answer, Mia ran across the room and launched herself at them. Isabelle caught her up in her arms and hugged tight.

"Mama, did you see? Aunt Jess finally came home. Chance found her."

Isabelle glanced at Adam and then at Jess and her husband. They all broke out laughing. She gazed up at Adam, at the love shining in his eyes, and sighed happily. "Thank you."

She set Mia down. "I'm sure Chance deserves a treat for that. Why don't you get him one?"

Mia scampered off, and Adam put his arm around Isabelle's shoulder. "Do I get a treat, too?"

She laughed and kissed him lightly on the cheek. "Will this do?"

"A little more to the left."

She grinned saucily and kissed him on the lips. "Better?"

"Only if you repeat it frequently." A sudden huskiness in his voice belied the joking tone of his words.

Isabelle laughed and shook her head. "Just like Chance and his treats." She reached up to rest her hand on his jaw and gazed deeply into his eyes, holding on to the promise of forever that shimmered there. "Whenever you want one," she murmured against his lips.

"In that case…" He lowered his head to hers and kissed her again.

Isabelle was vaguely aware of Mia clapping, and Jess and her husband cheering, but then Adam deepened his kiss and gathered her in his arms, and all she knew was the joy of his love.

* * * * *

Dear Reader,

When I began this book, I had *Beauty and the Beast* in mind, but as I researched the struggles veterans face, my story changed. The alarming rate of suicides and soldiers suffering PTSD shows the vicious toll war has taken on our veterans and their loved ones. I hope, through Adam and Isabelle, to show two faces of this battle: the veterans who suffer trauma from their service, and their families who cope with a loved one's struggle. My oldest daughter's experience with PTSD has taught me that while it has many causes and can wear many faces, it is a lifelong fight.

Fortunately, due to increasing awareness, many unique programs have been designed to help returning warriors. Wilderness therapy and therapy dogs are just two examples of the innovative types of treatment available to those who seek help.

My prayers go to all who are on this journey to life and healing.

Blessings,
Cate